Greek Island Brides

Finding love that lasts to infinity!

All marriages that take place on renowned wedding destination Infinity Island are guaranteed to last forever!

And the picturesque Greek island is about to weave its magic for friends Lea, Popi and Stasia. They dream of finding their own happily-ever-afters... And they're about to meet three billionaires who will sweep them off their feet—and down the aisle!

Follow Lea's journey from surprise pregnancy to dream proposal in

Carrying the Greek Tycoon's Baby

And discover Popi's journey from surrogate to unexpected mom in

Claiming the Drakos Heir

Both available now!

Look out for Stasia's story

Coming soon!

Dear Reader,

Even in the deepest, darkest of tragedies, a tiny miracle can occur. And from that miracle, healing can begin. At least that's what happens with Popi and Apollo.

When a freak accident kills Popi's adopted sister and brother-in-law, she is left carrying her sister's baby. Agreeing to be a surrogate had been a big decision for Popi and one she hadn't taken lightly. And now that her sister is gone, it is up to Popi to step up and raise the child of her heart.

Just when Popi has begun making plans for a family, the baby's globe-trotting uncle shows up on Infinity Island. He's there to claim his niece or nephew, but the baby has yet to be born. In an effort to honor their siblings' memories, both Popi and Apollo want custody of the child. With Apollo being the biological relative, he thinks he has an edge, but Popi believes that it takes more than a blood link to make a family. She believes it takes love, time and devotion.

However, they soon learn that it's going to take both of them to bring this precious bundle into the world. One night when the lights go out during a horrific storm, they have to learn to trust each other. There's no other way to deliver a healthy baby. But will that trust last after the sun comes up? And will baby make three?

Happy reading,

Jennifer

Claiming the Drakos Heir

—

Jennifer Faye

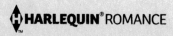
HARLEQUIN® ROMANCE

Recycling programs
for this product may
not exist in your area.

ISBN-13: 978-1-335-49940-0

Claiming the Drakos Heir

First North American publication 2019

Copyright © 2019 by Jennifer F. Stroka

Printed in U.S.A.

Award-winning author **Jennifer Faye** pens fun, heartwarming contemporary romances with rugged cowboys, sexy billionaires and enchanting royalty. Internationally published, with books translated into nine languages, she is a two-time winner of the *RT Book Reviews* Reviewers' Choice Award. She has also won the CataRomance Reviewers' Choice Award, been named a Top Pick author and been nominated for numerous other awards.

Books by Jennifer Faye

Harlequin Romance

Greek Island Brides

Carrying the Greek Tycoon's Baby

The Cattaneos' Christmas Miracles

Heiress's Royal Baby Bombshell

Once Upon a Fairytale

Beauty and Her Boss
Miss White and the Seventh Heir

Mirraccino Marriages

The Millionaire's Royal Rescue
Married for His Secret Heir

Her Festive Baby Bombshell
Snowbound with an Heiress

Visit the Author Profile page
at Harlequin.com for more titles.

Praise for
Jennifer Faye

"I still can't believe it's been this long since I read [Harlequin Romance]. Not to mention, Ms. Faye.... I just fell in love with this family and I can't wait to get my paperback copies of Leo and Sebastian's stories. Perfect for Christmas."

—*Harlie's Books* on *Heiress's Royal Baby Bombshell*

CHAPTER ONE

TODAY WAS THE WEDDING.

And nothing was going to go wrong.

Popi Costas assured herself that all would be well on this gorgeous autumn day. After all, she'd gone over every detail at least a dozen times. This was the most important wedding that she'd ever planned—even topping the royal wedding they'd hosted earlier that year.

This was the last wedding on Infinity Island before the groom, Xander, brought in work crews to give the private Greek island a much-needed facelift. In fact, they'd been having all the residents pack up their things so they could be put into storage while the renovations took place.

In the meantime, Popi planned to visit with her parents until the work on the island was complete. And after all the misery they'd faced that summer, they all needed some happiness. She could barely believe two months had passed since her adopted sister and brother-in-law had been alive in one breath...

And gone in the next.

How had it all gone so wrong? Popi had asked herself that question countless times. And she'd never come up with a sufficient answer. All she knew was what she'd been told—her sister and brother-in-law had died in a boating accident.

Something had triggered an explosion and no one had escaped the blazing inferno in the middle of the sea. It felt as though a piece of Popi had died along with them. If only she'd have said something… Done something…

She halted her thoughts. Today was about her best friend, Lea, getting married to the love of her life. If two people ever belonged together, it was the two of them—

Knock-knock.

Popi lowered the curling iron she'd been using to put elegant barrel rolls in her long hair. With only half her hair curled, she really didn't need any interruptions right now. If it was Lea, she would let herself inside. So it had to be someone else. Maybe if she ignored her unwanted guest, they would go away. Yes, that sounded like a good plan.

Popi sectioned off more hair and rolled it onto the iron. She needed to get to the reception as soon as possible to make sure everything was in place. Even though she'd just been there less than two hours ago and gone over the plans with the staff for the umpteenth time, she still worried something would go astray.

She didn't know why she was so nervous. She planned weddings for a living—big ones, small ones, traditional, original and everything in between. But this wedding was for her dearest friend. And Popi needed it to go off without a hitch.

Just then the baby kicked. Being almost nine months pregnant with her niece or nephew added a whole new level of turbulent emotions to the situation. When she'd agreed to be the surrogate for her sister, she never imagined life could be so cruel and at the same time provide such a precious blessing—a little piece of her sister lived on.

Popi placed a protective hand over her abdomen. "Don't worry, little one. I will make sure you are safe and loved."

Popi unrolled the iron. She never considered becoming a parent while she was still in her twenties, but there was no way she would turn her back on her sister's baby. Though she tried to put on a brave face, on the inside she was worried about being a good parent. She'd been reading parenting books but would it be enough?

Her life was about to change in so many ways, as the baby was due in a couple of weeks. Not long at all—

Knock-knock. Knock-knock.

So much for ignoring them.

"Anyone home?" A male voice called out through the open window.

Who could that be?

Popi wasn't expecting anyone. Everyone she knew was getting ready for the wedding. And then the thought of something going wrong with the wedding had her rushing out of the bathroom in her fluffy, short pink robe that barely fit over her baby bump and with a large portion of her hair pulled up in a big orange clip.

Popi swung the door open. Her gaze took in the man's scruffy but sexy appearance. From his longish hair to the thick scruff trailing along his dark, tanned jawline—his slack jaw, as though he'd opened his mouth to say something but totally forgot what it was he'd been meaning to say.

His casual white shirt and cargo shorts let her know he wasn't one of the wedding guests. Nor did he work on the island, as she knew everyone. That meant he must have been hired to help with the island renovations. But what was he doing here today?

When her gaze returned to his face, she noticed his rounded eyes were blue—not just blue, but a light blue that caught and held her attention. But his gaze wasn't meeting hers. In fact, his gaze was aimed southward.

His Adam's apple bobbed. "You're pregnant."

She stifled a laugh at his obvious discomfort. Had this man never seen a pregnant woman before? Or was she so large now that it bordered on the obscene?

Popi pressed a hand to the small of her back, trying to ease the ache. "You win the gold star for the day. I am indeed pregnant. Very pregnant." And then realizing that by putting her hand behind her back that her fuzzy robe was straining to cover all her amplified curves, she immediately lowered her arm to her side.

Was it just her or did the man look distinctly pale? Not like he hadn't seen any sun recently, because he most definitely had a better tan than her, but rather his face had drained of its color.

Struggling not to squirm under his bold stare, she asked, "What can I do for you?"

He cleared his throat and raised his gaze until those dreamy blue eyes finally stared into her own. "Are you Popi?"

"I am."

"I don't know if you were expecting me—"

"I wasn't." The movers weren't scheduled to arrive until tomorrow to transfer her belongings to storage. "Today is a really bad day for me." It was the worst day for a surprise. Her focus was supposed to be on Lea, not anything else. But apparently this very strong, very handsome stranger hadn't gotten the message.

He had broad shoulders and his shirt clung to his muscled chest, while the short sleeves wrapped snuggly around his bulging biceps. One arm had a tattoo of a map of the world overlaid with a compass. From the looks of this man, he didn't believe in spending much time indoors. And the sun gods had blessed him with strength and the most amazing tan that accentuated the lines of his muscles.

Popi swallowed hard. Maybe she'd been too focused on her problems lately to notice what was around her. Or else it was the pregnancy hormones. But this guy looked good enough to serve up on the top of a wedding cake.

Realizing she was once again staring, Popi lifted her gaze, finding she had to crane her neck to meet his gaze. "You're early."

"Early?"

"Yes. You aren't supposed to be here until tomorrow. I have a wedding today." But it wouldn't hurt to get a move on the work, since she hadn't finished packing, and she wanted to get to the mainland and her parents' house by tomorrow evening.

Confusion reflected in his eyes. "I didn't know about any wedding. No one mentioned it." Then his brows lifted. "Are you getting married?"

She couldn't help but laugh. Her irritation with him drained away. "Not a chance. It's my best friend's wedding and I'm coordinating it."

"Oh." He looked caught off guard and unsure what to say or do next.

"No worries." She stepped back. "Come on in.

You can move all the boxes out of the guest room and stack them here in the living room. They'll be ready for pickup in the morning."

"You want them moved now?"

"Yes."

The man's face creased with worry lines, but she didn't have time to answer whatever questions he had. How many questions could there be to move boxes from one room to the next?

She checked the time on her watch. "I have to hurry."

"But—"

"I can't answer questions now. If it's too much for you, you'll have to come back tomorrow." She turned for the master suite. No moving man, no matter how hot she found him, was going to hold her up. She had a bride waiting for her.

CHAPTER TWO

WHAT JUST HAPPENED?

Apollo Drakos stood slack-jawed as the woman sashayed down the hallway, but to be honest her sashay was more like a waddle. A cute waddle, but still a waddle all the same.

How could she still be pregnant?

His attorney had assured him the baby was born, though no one had been able to tell him if it was a boy or girl. Not that it mattered to him. Either way, he was still claiming his niece or nephew.

The attorney had gone on to inform him that Miss Costas would have a strong case to gain full custody of the baby, as well as control over the child's inheritance. The attorney even seemed to think that with Miss Costas being adopted and not the child's biological aunt, it wouldn't be enough to sway the judge from giving her custody. But did Popi really want to take on that responsibility? Or was she doing it out of necessity?

Apollo knew he had no one to blame for this

mess but himself. While Popi had been here, help-ing to make his brother and sister-in-law's dream of a family into a reality, he'd been off on another adventure—avoiding the fact that he was the un-wanted son, the outcast. But he'd come here as soon as he'd heard. That had to count for some-thing, didn't it?

But how was this going to work now that he knew Popi was still pregnant? Although it did look as though she was going to give birth soon. Not that he was an expert on pregnant women. Yet all of her was thin except for her stomach. It was very round indeed. Funnily enough, from behind you couldn't even tell she was pregnant. However, the cute little waddle did give it away.

It wasn't until now—seeing Popi round with a baby—that he realized how much she'd done for his brother and sister-in-law. Not everyone would step up and offer to carry someone else's baby—certainly not him, if that were even a possibility.

Gathering himself, Apollo pressed his lips to-gether in a firm line. Who exactly did this woman think he was? And where was she moving to with his brother's baby?

The baby belonged at the Drakos estate, which was situated just outside Athens. It was a place Apollo rarely visited. Though the vast estate was aesthetically beautiful, it held many dark memo-ries. When Apollo was a kid, it felt more like a prison he so desperately wanted to escape. While his older brother, Nile, had been cast as the "good son," Apollo had been labelled "worthless" by their father.

Apollo slammed the door on the bad memories. But no matter how many times he turned his back on the past, the door would eventually creak open once more. He'd heard it said that you can't outrun the past. He should know—he'd been trying for years and it was still just a blink away.

He needed to concentrate on the here and now. Everything was such an utter mess. If only he'd have come home when his brother had asked…

But being away on a two-month hiking expedition in the Himalayas, he'd been out of contact with the entire world—including his older brother, Nile. At the time, Apollo found it so freeing. A chance to let go of the ghosts of the past and embrace the present. At the time, he'd had no idea how much that freedom would cost him.

When he'd returned to civilization, he'd been unconscious, injured and alone. By the time he'd been able to speak on the phone, he'd had no one to call about his accident because his brother had been furious with him during their final phone conversation. After surgery and therapy for his broken leg, a private investigator had tracked him down at the hospital. It was then that he'd received the worst news of his life.

His big, strong, protective brother was dead.

Apollo's footloose and carefree life had come to an end in that moment.

All of the things that he'd put off—all of the words that he'd hesitated to say to Nile— the overdue apology, the thank-you, the *I love you, brother*—the chance to say any of it had slipped through his fingers. His brother would never know what he meant to him—how much he longed to mend their relationship.

In that moment, Apollo had never felt so alone in his life.

And then in the next breath, the investigator had informed him that he had a niece or nephew. Apollo's heart had leapt. There was another Drakos in this world. He wasn't alone.

He had one last chance to make it up to his brother for cutting loose and leaving home all those years ago. He'd let Nile deal with all the Drakos' business and their father. But on one sunny afternoon, his brother's life had been cut incredibly short, as was his sister-in-law's.

A boating accident. Who dies while boating?

It seemed unreal. So implausible. And yet the sharp pain of loss was quite real. And to add salt to the wound, it had happened almost two months ago. His brother and sister-in-law had been laid to rest and Apollo hadn't been there for any of it because no one knew where he was…except his brother.

He'd once again let down Nile. But that

wouldn't happen again. He was on Infinity Island to retrieve his niece or nephew…even if it meant he had to wait for its very precious arrival.

Apollo's thoughts turned back to Popi. He knew she'd been through a lot—he knew better than anyone. How would she react when she learned he was there for the baby?

Maybe she'd filed for custody of the baby because she didn't think he'd want to take responsibility for the baby. Maybe once he explained things to her, she'd realize the baby belonged with him, where the child would be groomed to take over the Drakos empire. Could it really be that simple? Would Popi hand the baby over to him like she'd been planning to do with his brother and her sister?

Apollo thought about following her to the back of the bungalow and reasoning with her. But then he recalled that little pink robe. He swallowed hard. Did she realize it barely covered her? It was so tantalizing, hinting at the curvy goodness that lay beneath. But the robe never really revealed anything scandalous. It was more the knowledge that she didn't have a thing on underneath that turned his blood red-hot.

He tugged on his shirt collar. It was a bit warm out, even with the sea breeze. His mind was still replaying the images of Popi. He'd gotten a good view of her shapely legs. They were long and smooth. His mouth grew dry. Why did this woman have to be so good-looking? It was a distraction that he didn't need or want.

His back teeth ground together. He had to get past the superficial. His purpose for coming to the island couldn't be forgotten. If he stayed focused, he would soon forget about Popi's finer assets. At least he hoped so.

Apollo walked back out the front door. He started down the steps with no particular destination in mind. He didn't even know anything about this island, except that the woman who was carrying his last living relative lived here.

He came to a stop and turned. Why was he walking away? Maybe because that's what he'd been doing his whole life. But no more.

Apollo returned to the porch and took a seat in one of the two wicker chairs. They looked stiff and uninviting, but once he was seated, he found them surprisingly comfortable. He lounged back and decided to learn more about Infinity Island. He pulled out his phone and typed the name into the search engine.

He was surprised by the large number of articles written about the island. In his limited experience with women, he knew it may take Popi quite some time to get ready. He settled back in the chair, pulled up the first article about this "wedding" island and started to read.

To his surprise there was a picture of Popi, smiling at the camera. She was arm and arm with another woman. He wondered if this was today's bride. The caption beneath the photo said that the other woman was the owner, while Popi was the wedding planner.

Apollo inwardly groaned. This woman believed in hearts, flowers and happily-ever-afters. Those were things he'd purposely avoided all his adult life. What exactly had he gotten himself into? Maybe he should have let his army of attorneys handle it. But he didn't want to put either of them through a long, drawn-out legal battle. They'd already been through so much—especially Popi.

And so he kept reading about the island. The more he knew, the easier it would be to reason with her, should it come to that. After all, the heir to the Drakos fortune couldn't be raised in a hut on some small, out-of-the-way island…

A movement out of the corner of his eye had him glancing up. In a whirl of coral gauzy material, and with long brown curls bouncing, Popi walked swiftly away from the bungalow. Apparently she hadn't noticed him sitting off to the side.

He got to his feet and slipped the phone in his pocket, but in just that small amount of time she'd darted down a path. The problem was there were a lot of paths, and he wasn't sure which one she'd gone down. How could a very pregnant woman move so quickly?

He knew she was busy with the wedding, but after it was over, perhaps at the reception, he could grab a moment of her time. He just wanted her to know he was here now. She didn't have to go through the remainder of this pregnancy alone.

CHAPTER THREE

SHE DIDN'T NEED any more complications.

Popi made a mental note to let the supervisor in charge of the move know about the man showing up at her bungalow on the wrong day. And on top of it, the man hadn't done anything she'd instructed him to do. In fact, the man had done absolutely nothing. He better not even try to charge time for today. She wouldn't stand for it.

Popi headed straight for the Hideaway Café. She refused to let herself get utterly distracted by that man—no matter how sexy he was with those mesmerizing blue eyes and that intriguing tattoo on his bicep. She halted her thoughts. She had a very important wedding today. Everything else would have to wait until another time—including the mystery man.

Popi came to a stop on the patio of the café. This was Lea's dream wedding spot. It had the most awesome view of the bay, but as beautiful as the view was, it wasn't Popi's vision for saying "I do." Whenever she got married, she loved the idea of a lush garden. Intimate and yet with hundreds of colorful blooms in every shade imaginable.

Popi paused to take in the view. She'd worked closely with Lea to plan this wedding down to the finest detail. Lea had told her not to push so hard, but Popi needed to focus on the wedding. Working was her way of dealing with the loss of her sister. The work kept her grounded when everything around her felt as though it was spinning out of control.

All the outdoor white tables with their colorful umbrellas had been removed to make room for rows of white folding chairs. Lea had opted for wildflowers, which included locally grown orchids. Popi hadn't been sure about the idea, but now seeing them in arrangements throughout the venue, she had to admit it looked stunning.

There was little more than an hour until the wedding—time that would be needed to get the bride ready. Though Lea had moved to the island little more than a year ago, she was embracing the Greek culture, and the older women on the island had filled Lea's head with all the wedding traditions. Lea was excited to merge some of the old ways with some of her own traditions. It would make for a beautiful wedding.

After inspecting the venue preparations, Popi took off for Lea's bungalow. Thankfully there was a golf cart at the offices. She planned to acquire it, as her feet were getting tired and the event hadn't even begun. Carrying around an extra human was taxing.

She placed a hand on her aching lower back. "Not that I'd have it any other way. We'll make your parents proud."

She sat in the cart and then set off down the familiar path. One of the first Greek traditions they'd dealt with was setting the wedding date. When the elders on the island had heard the wedding was to be in August, they immediately spoke up. They advised that if the wedding must be in August, then the first two weeks of the month should be avoided at all costs, as they were reserved for religious reasons.

Neither Lea nor Popi were very religious, but, they reasoned, why tempt fate and the ire of the elders? As such, they planned the wedding for the last weekend in the month. Everyone seemed pleased with the decision, as Xander had arranged for a cruise ship to take everyone from the island for a Mediterranean cruise right after the reception.

The plan was, while they were all off on a two-week cruise, followed by temporary lodgings in Athens, the island would undergo extensive renovations. When the citizens were allowed to return to their bungalows, everything would be updated and the crews would be out of their way. It was quite an amazing gift from the bridegroom to his new extended family.

A couple of minutes later, Popi pulled to a stop in front of Lea's bungalow. The bridegroom wasn't there. He was bunking with the island's handyman, Joseph, until the wedding. In the time Xander had been on the island, the older man had taken him under his wing, like a father would do.

When Popi entered the bungalow, she was surprised to find so many women rushing around. But she didn't see Lea among them. And then her name was called. She glanced around, finding Lea waving her to the guest room.

Popi made her way to Lea. Once inside the room, she closed the door. "What are you doing in here instead of your room?"

Lea rolled her eyes. "The elders are so caught up in the wedding. They think my soon-to-be husband is in line to be a saint for all he's doing for them that they don't want to jinx anything."

"Do I dare ask what that means?"

"They're preparing the marital bed... Um... what did they call it? Oh, yes, *to krevati*."

"What?" She'd heard of the tradition but she'd never heard of anyone actually doing it. "You mean like with the rose petals, ribbons and money?"

"And rice. Don't forget the rice. They've been here cleaning and putting fresh linens on the bed. I had to talk them out of rolling an infant on the bed. I told them we didn't need any help in the fertility department." Lea ran a loving hand over her own expanding midsection.

Popi burst out laughing. "Definitely not. But they could have just rolled you around on the bed."

"Don't give them any ideas." Lea shook her head. "So I've been hiding in here."

"You don't have time to hide. It isn't long until you say 'I do.' I'll just go get some makeup and I'll be right back."

Popi was the maid of honor, or *koumbara*, and it was her responsibility to see that the bride was ready on time. The rest of the bridal party soon showed up, including Lea's assistant and her soon to be sister-in-law, Stasia. Because an odd number of attendants was good luck. And three attendants were the best.

Together they worked until Lea was all done up with her long hair pulled up with just a few strategically placed curly wisps of hair softening her face. A wreath of fresh flowers was clipped into place.

Popi stepped back and took in Lea's dress. It was truly breathtaking. White tiers of Chantilly lace, tulle and ribbons adorned her. There was a V-shaped neckline with delicate straps over her shoulders and satin ribbon wrapped around her waist. She truly looked like a Greek goddess.

"You're perfect," Popi announced. And the other young women readily agreed.

"Not quite." Lea slipped off her white heels.

"What are you doing?" Popi frowned. "Is it your shoes? Is something wrong with them?"

Lea shook her head. "Does someone have a pen?"

"I do." Stasia pulled a fine black marker from her purse.

Popi watched as Lea wrote the names of her bridal party on the bottom of her shoes. Lea had written her name first, before Popi could tell her not to do it. It was another Greek tradition that the names of the single ladies be written on the bottom of the bride's shoes. The names that are worn off by the end of the evening will soon be married. Popi was certain that her name would still be there, because there was no chance she was getting married anytime soon. She already had her hands more than full with the little bundle of joy inside her.

As though the baby sensed her thoughts, it kicked. Once. Twice. And the last kick was swifter than the others, sending Popi bending over. She pressed a hand to the area where she'd been kicked.

"Are you okay?" Lea asked, concern written all over her face, as well as the other ladies.

Popi drew in a deep, soothing breath and

straightened. "Yeah. I think I have a footballer in there."

"Oh." Lea smiled.

"Don't smile," Popi said. "Your time is coming."

Lea continued to smile as she pressed a hand to her baby bump. "It'll all be worth it in the end."

Popi smiled. "You just keep telling yourself that when the baby starts tap-dancing on your bladder."

Lea's smile dimmed. "I hadn't thought of that."

Knock-knock.

Popi went to the door and opened it a crack. On the other side was the photographer. After glancing around to make sure the coast was clear of the groom, Popi admitted the photographer. It was almost time to head to the Hideaway.

After today, their lives were going to change dramatically. Her friend would be married, with a baby created from that love already on the way. It didn't get any better than that. Popi was so happy for her—for all of them.

Sometimes Popi wondered if the baby she was carrying would feel like they'd missed out on something by not having a father. But then again, they most certainly would feel cheated by never knowing either of their biological parents. A sadness filled Popi. If only she could change the past.

She recalled her last conversation with her sister. Neither suspected it would be the last time they spoke. And the conversation had gone totally sideways.

Popi blamed herself for the heated exchange... for Andrina and Nile being on that boat at that particular time...for them needlessly dying. Popi's throat tightened. Her breath caught in her lungs. If only she'd said something different—if she'd had more patience—then they'd both still be alive. If that conversation had gone differently, her sister and brother-in-law would be here, anxiously awaiting the arrival of their first child. She was positive of it.

The photographer bumped into her, jarring her from the emotional black hole that threatened to swallow her whole. The man turned to her. "Sorry. Would you mind helping the bride with her hair so I can get a few photos?"

Not trusting her voice, Popi nodded.

Today was not the time to contemplate her sister's death. Today was about smiles, hopes and good tidings. Popi choked down all her worries and smiled. Lea deserved nothing but happiness on her big day.

He didn't want to be here.

But on this small island, places to wait for Popi were limited. And the wedding appeared to be taking place in a common area of the village.

Apollo found himself standing off to the side.

No one seemed to make a big deal of him being there. They acted as though he was just another wedding guest. Some even shook his hand and greeted him.

Up until now, Apollo had done nothing but make one mistake after the next since the day he was born. He thought he'd have time to fix things—to change his ways. After all, he was young. There was plenty of time to make up for the past, but then suddenly out of nowhere he'd been blindsided when time had run out for Nile and his wife, Andrina. And now he owed it to his brother not to mess things up where the baby was concerned.

As he thought of Nile, the breath hitched in Apollo's throat. It wasn't supposed to happen this way. He was the adventure seeker—the daredevil. If something bad had to happen, it should have been to him. Not his brother. None of this made any sense.

A flurry of motion drew Apollo from his thoughts. The wedding guests took their seats. Not wanting to stand out any more than he already did with his casual attire, Apollo took a seat in the back. The classical music started. Two pretty women started up the aisle.

And then Popi appeared at the end of the aisle, holding a bouquet of teal blossoms. She looked radiant. Her smile lit up her whole face. All he could do in that minute was stare at the most beautiful woman he'd ever seen in his life. It was the same sort of stunned reaction he'd experienced at her place, when he'd found her in the very short, very revealing pink robe. He couldn't decide which look he preferred on her. Both looks had their alluring qualities.

It was in that moment her gaze lifted, meeting his. The breath caught in his chest. Her big brown eyes were mesmerizing. He felt as though he were being drawn into her chocolate-brown depths. His heart beat faster, as time felt as though it had been suspended.

She was looking right at him as she stepped forward. His mouth grew dry. He should turn away, but he couldn't. She was amazing in every way.

And then she passed by him and kept going to where the priest and groom waited. Apollo didn't take an easy breath until the bride moved to the end of the aisle.

The wedding proceeded slowly and they had finally come to the blessing of the rings. The wedding bands were exchanged three times. Apollo rolled his shoulders. He willed the wedding to hurry up and end, but they were just now taking three sips of wine as a symbol of sharing for the rest of their marriage. He'd forgotten about three being such a significant number in Greek culture.

When they made it to the traditional readings, he resisted the urge to squirm in his seat. He'd done far too much sitting on planes in order to get to this little, out-of-the-way island as fast as he could. And his injuries were not taking all the sitting in one position well.

When the ceremony finally ended and the guests were directed to the garden area next to the café where the reception was being held, Apollo fell in step with everyone else. He was surprised when he only received a few odd glances at his choice of casual attire. How was he supposed to know when he'd ventured to Infinity Island that his trip would include a wedding?

He kept trying to catch Popi alone, but she was forever talking with this person or that person. He just wanted a brief word with her. He hoped once she knew he wanted custody of the child that she'd withdraw her petition. And in the meantime, he'd pay for her medical expenses and anything else she needed. Could it be that simple?

Apollo didn't miss how Popi spoke to everyone she passed. There were a lot of hugs and smiles. Everyone was enjoying themselves. He was impressed with how this group of people could act like one big, happy, functional family, whereas his own blood relatives had never experienced anything close to this easiness with each other. Not that he ever needed a close-knit family. He did fine on his own.

Apollo's father had had two loves in his life while Apollo was growing up: the family business and his bottle of bourbon. Nile inherited their father's passion for the family business. Apollo never forgot Nile's obsession with all things Drakos. The thing Apollo never figured out was whether his brother's interest in the business was an effort to please their demanding father or if Nile just loved the business world to the exclusion of all else—until he'd met Andrina.

Everything had changed after Nile fell for Andrina. It was evident in his phone calls with his brother. Nile's voice had been full of happiness and he'd grown excited about the future, which was no longer centered on the business, but instead Nile was excited about the family he and Andrina were creating. However, Apollo didn't believe that happiness lasted.

And then he'd been proven right, again. The news of their deaths was like a one-two punch to the kidney. Emotionally it had knocked him out.

In a blink, his brother had been stolen away. Even now the pain of loss emanated outward from Apollo's chest. He didn't know how Popi was holding it all together—maybe it was due to the baby. She was being strong for it. He had to admire such strength and courage.

It was then that Popi approached him. And by her stiff posture, he was certain she was not happy about him crashing this wedding. Maybe this hadn't been such a great idea after all, but he was there now so he might as well stay and get this over with.

He was propped against a tall white column. He didn't move, as Popi was headed straight for him. "What are you doing here?" Her gaze narrowed. "You aren't part of the moving crew, are you?"

"Never said I was."

"But you let me believe you were."

"As I recall, you were in too much of a hurry to get the details."

Popi crossed her arms and glared at him. "Who are you?"

He cleared his throat. "I tried to tell you back at the bungalow—"

Just then there was the tinkle of a glass as people were called to take a seat for dinner. The bride motioned for Popi to join her at the head table.

Popi signaled that she was coming before she turned back to him. "I have to go."

Without waiting for him to respond, she turned her back to him and walked away. His gaze naturally followed the sway of her hips.

"This isn't over." The gentle breeze carried his words, but Popi was too far away to hear him.

He'd walked away from his brother, not intending for it to be forever, but that's exactly what had happened. He would never again speak to Nile, argue with him or take comfort in his brother's concern for his well-being. Without Nile, he utterly felt adrift in this great big world.

And then when he'd been informed about Nile's child—his last living link to his brother—Apollo knew in that moment that he had to set things right. Or as right as was possible. He owed Nile that much and so much more.

In the next breath, the attorney had informed him that Popi was seeking custody. If he didn't stop her, he would lose a tangible link to his brother—his only chance to do the right thing as far as his brother was concerned.

Apollo had vowed then and there to never walk away from the baby. It was all the family he had left. He would learn from his past and not make the same mistakes again—the stakes were too high.

Apollo was generally straightforward, but with a baby involved perhaps a gentler approach was in order. His father had been a very blunt man. Apollo knew how it felt to be on the receiving end of that bluntness. He wouldn't wish it on anyone.

Maybe a bit of charm and a few kind words would smooth the path to claiming his niece or nephew. He didn't know if it'd work, but it was worth a try. He didn't want to make this harder on Popi than it needed to be. But in the end, he intended for the baby to live with him at the Drakos estate.

CHAPTER FOUR

POPI BARELY ATE her dinner at the reception.

Her gaze kept moving over the crowd of well-wishers, searching for the strikingly handsome man. He seemed so familiar to her and yet she was certain they hadn't met before, but how could that be?

And what did he want with her? If he was a disgruntled client, he would want to speak with Lea, as she was the owner of the island and the wedding business. But Popi hadn't noticed a wedding ring on his finger.

Lea leaned over. "Is everything all right?"

Not wanting to alarm the bride on her big day, Popi said, "Yes, of course."

Lea's brows drew together. "Then why haven't you eaten?"

Popi glanced down. At one point, the food had looked appetizing, but now her stomach was a twisted-up ball of nerves. "I…um…was just distracted."

Lea arched a fine brow at her. "Distracted,

huh? With that handsome guy I saw you chatting with?"

Popi's gaze searched the area, not finding any sign of him. She didn't know what to say to Lea. She didn't want the bride worrying about the mystery man.

"Popi?"

She turned back to the bride. "He's, um, with the movers. There was some kind of mix-up and he showed up a day early. I hope him crashing the wedding hasn't upset you."

A look of disappointment skittered across Lea's face. "So he wasn't here at your invitation?"

Popi gave a firm shake of her head.

"I'll have him escorted off the island—"

"No. Don't." There was something about his serious tone and the feeling she should know him that had her anxious to learn his story. "I've got it."

Lea looked hesitant. "You're sure?"

Popi nodded. The truth was she wasn't sure about anything—especially why this man was so eager to speak with her.

Lea let the subject drop. And with the mystery man now gone, Popi forced herself to eat a few bites of food. The evening moved along with the groom, Xander, dancing the traditional *zeibekiko*. The crowd clapped as Xander's arms rose over his head. He snapped his fingers as he moved in a tight circle. He stopped in front of

Lea and dropped to his knees, still waving his arms over his head. The crowd loved it, most especially Lea. The smile on the bride's face lit up the whole room.

One dance led to another. The bride and groom were all smiles, as they had eyes only for each other. Popi considered this wedding a success. She took her first easy breath.

And the next thing she knew, she was being led around the dance floor by the best man, Roberto, who was also Xander's close friend and second-in-command. She'd met him more than once, and though Lea was anxious for them to hit it off, it wasn't going to happen. Popi couldn't put her finger on why. He was definitely handsome and successful, but neither one was into the other. They were becoming fast friends, but that's all it would ever be.

Partway through the song, there was a tap on Roberto's shoulders. Popi's gaze followed the finger up the arm and then her gaze settled upon the sexy stranger's face. Apparently it was time for their talk. She had to admit that she was anxious to learn his identity and what he had to tell her.

"Can I cut in?" The stranger wore a serious expression.

Roberto, looking caught off guard, stopped dancing. "Um…" His gaze moved to her and she nodded. "Thank you for the dance." Roberto turned back to the other man. "She's all yours."

The man took Popi in his quite capable arms, but there was no escaping their closeness with her protruding abdomen. No one had long enough arms to allow for much room between them— not even this man.

"What are you doing?" Her voice came out in a heated whisper.

"Dancing. With you." He led her around the dance floor.

"But I don't know your name. I don't even understand why you're at the wedding—"

"Shh… I'll answer all your questions after one dance. That seems like a fair bargain, doesn't it?" He smiled at her, but it didn't quite reach his eyes.

His words were smooth, but she got the impression there was more going on here than him trying to pick her up. Although, a man with his striking good looks being interested in dancing with a woman almost nine months pregnant was an offer she couldn't turn down.

She nodded her consent.

His muscled arm moved to her waist while he took her hand in his and held it to his chest. Her heart was racing madly. She assured herself it was the physical activity and nothing to do with the handsome man holding her in his arms.

His gaze met hers and held it. She wasn't able to read his thoughts, but that didn't keep her heart from continuing to race. Was it wrong to acknowledge that he was the sexiest man at the wedding? On the *island*?

As she stared into his blue eyes, she was caught off guard by a glimmer of pain lurking just beneath the surface. Normally when she looked into someone's eyes, there was a light there, but in this mysterious stranger's case, it was as if that light had been snuffed out. Someone had hurt him— hurt him deeply. Sympathy welled up in her. She was all too familiar with pain that balled up inside and made it difficult to eat, sometimes to inhale a full breath.

He glanced away, breaking the contact. So he wasn't into sharing either, not that it was any of her business. But she couldn't help but be intrigued by him. Again, she was struck by his familiarity, but she was certain they hadn't previously met. There was no way that she would forget someone as good-looking as him.

The song playing in the background was a classic: "Moondance." As the singer's deep voice wafted through the air, Popi's dance partner guided her around the crowded dance floor. White twinkle lights were strung overhead, casting a soft glow over the area.

But all Popi had eyes for was the handsome man holding her in his arms as though she belonged there. For just this moment, reality, with all its sorrow, rolled away.

When his gaze met hers once more, there was

something different reflected in his blue eyes. Was it interest? In her? Her heart skipped a beat. How could he desire her in her current condition? Impossible. Wasn't it?

For this one dance, she allowed herself the luxury of pretending that he was her lover. What could it hurt? It'd been so very long since she'd felt anything but the heavy weight of guilt and the darkness of grief.

For this one dance beneath the starry sky, she'd allow herself to be happy.

It'd been a long time since he'd danced.

And he was surprised to find he enjoyed holding Popi close.

Realizing he was enjoying it too much, Apollo guided them off to a quiet corner of the dance floor. His intent was to have a serious conversation with her, but this close contact was detrimental to his thought process.

He drew in a deep breath, but it did nothing to cool his heated blood. There was something about this woman that got past his practiced defenses. And right now, talking was the last thing on his mind.

Blindly following his desires was how he'd gotten himself into a number of jams in the past, from angry fathers with shotguns to returning to camp, where a tribal leader and anxious bride awaited him. He was older now, more responsible. But that didn't make Popi any less enchanting.

Get it together. He mustered up an image of the legal documents—papers that would steal away his last link to his brother. Suddenly his heated blood cooled and his thoughts became more focused.

And then he turned his gaze back to Popi. Perhaps he'd made a miscalculation by lingering at this wedding. He should have waited to speak with her. But he'd already waited too long to take his rightful place in the Drakos family. Guilt and determination kept him from walking away.

If only Popi didn't look so captivating, he'd be able to sort his thoughts—to speak his mind. His gaze continued to take in her beauty. Her hair was pinned up with just a few wispy strands of hair around her neck—ringlets that teased and tempted him to reach out and wrap them around his finger. And her gown hugged her curves and dipped low enough to hint at her tempting cleavage.

His mouth grew dry and his hands grew damp. Testosterone challenged his common sense. She looked so fine—very different from his sister-in-law, whom he recalled being a lot less curvy and had portrayed a more serious demeanor. And his old self would have swept Popi off her feet by now. It was so difficult being responsible and doing what was proper when his entire body longed to do all those improper things with Popi.

He blamed this instant attraction on this island. His research had unearthed that Infinity Island was famous for its romances. Marriages started here were rumored to last forever. Was it possible that it did hold some sort of magical power? Instead of a love potion, perhaps the island cast a love spell over its inhabitants.

Because right now, he was losing the struggle. All he could think about was kissing Popi. It didn't matter that they barely knew each other or that she was very, very pregnant. It was the way the moonlight was reflected in her eyes.

And then there was the way she looked at him when she hadn't thought he was paying attention. She was just as drawn to him as he was to her. That was the final part of his undoing.

Popi tilted her chin upward until their gazes met. "What's the matter?"

"In this moment, nothing."

"Then why did you stop dancing? Are you ready to answer my questions?"

He smiled at her tenacity, but he wasn't ready to ruin this moment with the harshness of reality. It would happen soon enough. He drew her close again as the remaining verses of the song played. He heard the swift intake of her breath as her eyes widened. "The song isn't quite over."

Their bodies swayed together, but their feet didn't move.

He lowered his head to her ear. Softly he said, "Do you know how beautiful you are?"

And then without thinking of the consequences—the right and wrong—he turned his head. He caught her lips. Part of him expected her to pull away—another part of him willed her to meet him halfway.

And then her mouth moved beneath his. His heart slammed into his ribs. Her glossy lips moved with eagerness. His tongue sought entrance. Her mouth widened, causing a moan to swell in the back of his throat.

Was this really happening? Could this amazing woman really be this into him? In that moment, he couldn't think of anything he wanted more than her.

Being alone for so long—just him and nature—it got so lonely at times. Not that he'd ever admitted it to anyone. But with Popi in his arms, he had a glimpse of what life might be like if he were to let someone get close.

Her hand reached up and wrapped around his neck. In that moment, he lost his fingertip-hold on reality. Popi leaned into him. Her lips moved over his, taking the lead in this arousing dance. She was so hot that everywhere she touched him, he felt singed. And he didn't want her to stop.

He'd kept to himself for too long. He told himself that was why her kiss was sweeter than the passion fruit Moscato wine being passed around the wedding. He assured himself it was all an illusion that would soon pass. But the longer they kissed, the more he craved her.

Apollo let go of her hand to wrap his arm around her waist. Her baby bump kept him from being able to pull her as close as he would like. It was a reminder that this wasn't a fantasy. Popi was very much flesh and blood.

He should stop this. He should put some distance between them. He took a small step back—at least he thought it was a step—but Popi was still leaning into him as their lips moved hungrily over each other.

Her fingers spread out over his chest, scattering his thoughts of ending things. The V-neck of his shirt allowed her fingertips to touch his bare skin. It was as though just by her touch alone, she branded him as her own.

No woman, no kiss, had ever affected him so deeply. It was like they'd been made for each other. She was the half that made him whole.

A drum roll echoed through the garden and pounded reality back into his head. He pulled back and looked at her. It took them each a moment to catch their breath. He hadn't come here to kiss Popi. His fingers moved over his mouth, still remembering the softness of her touch. He drew in an uneven breath.

Kissing her had been a mistake. He didn't know if he was going to be able to talk to her—to look at her—without recalling that earth-moving kiss. And he couldn't afford to be distracted. There was too much at stake.

He stepped away. "That shouldn't have happened."

Popi's gaze darkened. "The song has ended. Now I want answers. Who are you?"

"Do you really not recognize me?"

"No." She studied his face. "Why should I know you? Are you famous?"

"In a manner of speaking." He'd been fodder for the tabloids off and on his whole life. Billionaire heir spotted here…spotted there. "I'm Apollo Drakos."

Her mouth gaped. Her eyes reflected the rampant thoughts racing through her mind. It took her a moment to press her glossy lips together.

Popi's gaze narrowed. "Where have you been? We tried to reach you right after the accident, but no one knew what had happened to you."

"It doesn't matter—"

"Of course it matters." Her voice assumed an accusatory tone. "You should have been here."

His muscles tensed as yet another person heaped guilt on him. He deserved the condemnation and accusations, but there was nothing she could say that he hadn't already said to himself.

"I'm here now."

"Then you know about the accident and that we had the funeral—"

"I know all of it. My attorney filled me in."

Her gaze searched his. "Then what are you doing here on the island?"

"I'm here to claim the Drakos heir."

CHAPTER FIVE

NO. THAT CAN'T be true.

Popi's arms immediately wrapped around her midsection. She'd heard rumors about the man standing before her. Apollo was known to be reckless and selfish. No way was he going to steal away into the night with this baby. Not on her watch. But try as she might, the rush of words clogged up in her throat. The back of her eyes stung with tears of frustration and a flurry of hormones.

Popi's sister, Andrina, had said Apollo was a playboy—taking what he wanted and leaving a string of broken hearts across the globe. But Popi considered herself lucky. He'd stolen a kiss, not her heart.

Okay, maybe they'd shared much more than a fleeting kiss. But something had clicked between them when they'd been chest to heaving chest, lip to eager lip.

Maybe she'd let herself sympathize with the pain that had been reflected in his eyes. Maybe her own grief had her acting out of character. Whatever had her lip-dancing with him, it had nothing whatsoever to do with her heart.

She knew Mr. Globetrotter over there lived off his very large trust fund. He never put down roots anywhere. From all Popi had gathered, she had been certain he wouldn't want to complicate his carefree life with a baby.

And with her own parents getting older, they weren't up to the day-to-day care of a baby. That left her to raise her sister's child. And that's why she'd spoke with an attorney to get the adoption started.

"This surely can't come as a surprise," he said.

Her brows drew together in confusion. "You mean you showing up on the island unwanted and uninvited? Or did you mean you trying to charm me with your smooth words and kiss—"

"I wasn't trying to charm you. We both got caught up with the music and the dancing. It wasn't all one way." His pointed gaze met hers. When she opened her mouth to deny the accusation, he continued. "Don't bother. Remember I was on the other end of that kiss."

Wordlessly, she pressed her lips together. Perhaps it was best to pretend that kiss hadn't happened—for both of their sakes.

Though the music of the reception floated in the background, Popi was no longer in the mood to laugh and smile. Yes, she would have to go back to the party and put on a happy face, but not before she set a few things straight.

"You've wasted your time coming here," she said. "When this baby is born, I'm not going to allow you to walk away with it." Not a chance. She'd heard way too many stories about this guy, who acts first and thinks later. The baby wouldn't be safe with him.

He pressed his hands to this trim waist. "You can't stop me. I'm its uncle."

"I'm the aunt."

They stood quietly, glaring back and forth. Each waited for the other to back down. He'd be waiting a very long time, because she was never going to back down. This baby was too important.

From the stories she'd heard of Apollo, he had been a wild child. And as an adult, he did and said what he wanted without care to others. So why had he grown quiet? Why not say what he really thought? That she wasn't deserving of raising his niece or nephew, because secretly she had her own reservations. The guilt over her sister's death continued to eat at her.

Popi shoved aside the troubling thoughts. "You have some nerve coming here months after your brother and sister-in-law's deaths and throwing around demands. Where were you for the funeral?"

Apollo glanced down at the ground. She'd hit a nerve. Perhaps he wasn't as self-centered as her sister had let on. Perhaps there was a bit more to Apollo. But not enough to just turn the baby over to him. That wasn't going to happen, even if this man turned out to be a saint, which she knew he wasn't.

When her sister had first approached her about being a surrogate, Popi had outright rejected the idea. She'd thought she was too young to go through everything involved with pregnancy—not to mention the associated pain.

She'd told Andrina to find another way. Looking back, Popi felt so bad about giving her sister such a hard time. At the time, she hadn't known about her sister's repeated miscarriages that had devastated both Andrina and Nile. Her sister had held it all in, not wanting her family to know that she felt like a failure as a mother and wife. But when the news came out, not one of them thought any such thing.

When Andrina had finally let her guard down with Popi, something wonderful had happened. As Andrina had explained about the emotional roller coaster that she and Nile had been on, the sisters grew closer than they'd ever been before. Popi then saw the surrogacy in a new light—a chance to cement their relationship—to be more like blood siblings than two adopted orphans.

And this stranger wasn't going to walk in here after the fact and take away her last link to her sister. It just wasn't going to happen.

"Where have you been all of this time?" Popi hoped to drive home the fact that she had always been there. When her family needed her, she was there for them. Just like she'd be there when this baby needed her.

Apollo rubbed the back of his neck. And then in almost a mumble, he uttered a response, but it was too soft for Popi to pick it up over the sound of the music.

"What did you say?"

He lifted his head. In his eyes, she could see the torment reflected in them. For a moment, it stilled her breath. She didn't know what to do with this new information. It was so much easier to fight him when she thought he was a selfish jerk without any worry for anyone else.

"I was out of contact while hiking in the Himalayas."

That would explain the tan and the very defined muscles. And it would also explain his absence from the funeral. As much as she wanted to cling to his absence from that awful time, she could tell he was riddled with guilt over it. She knew a lot about being plagued with guilt.

But that didn't change the fact that she was better suited to be a parent. She had a job. A stable life. A home. And lots of caring people to help her raise this child. What was it they said? Oh, yes: it takes a village. And she was blessed enough to have a loving village.

What did he have?

Popi thought for a moment before speaking. She didn't want to escalate this situation. If she could reason with him, it would be best for everyone concerned—most especially the baby.

"I know you're concerned about the child." She noticed he didn't try to argue and so she continued. "I also know you lead a very active lifestyle, which isn't conducive to having an infant or a small child." When he started a rebuttal, she held up her hand, stopping him. "I also understand you might feel the pressure to do the right thing. But I want you to know that the right thing is to leave the baby with me to raise while you continue to explore the Amazon and hike the Himalayas or whatever."

His gaze narrowed in on her. "So that you can take control of the Drakos fortune?"

"What?" She knew her brother-in-law was rich—more than rich—but she never considered the money when she'd decided to adopt the baby. She never stopped to realize that the baby would be heir to a fortune. "No, that's not it."

Apollo's gaze said that he didn't believe her. "You will never get your hands on that money."

Her heart sunk. She thought Apollo had come here to claim the baby out of some sort of obligation or maybe even love for his brother. It never even occurred to her that this would be some sort of power move. A chance to control the family business that he'd been excluded from in favor of his older brother.

She shook her head in frustration. At that point, she could hear voices over the speaker system. It was time for the champagne toast, followed by the bridal-bouquet toss. Though Lea had been adamant about incorporating the Greek traditions in honor of her groom, she'd also introduced some American traditions and married them, as Lea liked to say.

"I have to go," Popi said. "In the future, your attorney can contact mine." And with that she walked away, not even waiting for him to speak.

Before Apollo's arrival, Popi had been determined to protect the child and keep it with her, and this conversation had only solidified her position. Apollo was going to walk away empty-handed.

That kiss.

Oh, that kiss.

Apollo inwardly groaned. It was the most arousing, addictive kiss of his life. And it had ended much, much too quickly. The fact that Popi had wanted him just as much had been a surprise.

As good as the kiss had been, it had been a mistake. And just when he'd promised himself that he was going to be responsible and do what was best for the family—for the baby. Because he owed it to his brother's memory.

And right about now, he was certain Nile would be frowning at him. He'd let his desires rule, but that was the last time. He didn't care how beautiful Popi was, as he could ignore her charms. He could be the responsible man his brother always believed he was capable of being.

That meant stepping up and becoming a father to his niece or nephew. The acknowledgment of that was immense.

But Apollo was done walking away.

He'd done that enough in his life.

This time he was staying. He would do what was right.

Being a father meant giving up his freedom. Nile would say that it was past time, and perhaps he was right after this latest accident. It had opened Apollo's eyes to what was important—family. He never got to tell his brother that—he never got to thank his brother for never giving up on him.

The only thing he could do now for his brother was to make sure his son or daughter was raised as a Drakos and received all the privileges that afforded them.

And that left Popi. Unlike her and her claim for sole custody, he would not exclude her from the child's life. He didn't know how exactly it would work, but he wouldn't exile Popi from the child she'd carried. There had to be a reasonable compromise. He just needed time to think.

It was late in the evening and Apollo was still on the island. In fact, he'd taken up residence on Popi's porch. He didn't like being dismissed. His father used to do it and it grated on Apollo's nerves.

He settled back in the chair and stared into the night. He recalled the determination written all over Popi's beautiful face when it came to raising the baby. But it wasn't going to stop him. He hadn't been there for his brother, but he was here now for his nephew or niece.

He'd already had the most highly recommended nanny put on retainer. She was just waiting for his word and she would move into his family's grand estate, just outside Athens. There was a very talented cook. And then there was Anna, the housekeeper. A smile tugged at his lips when he recalled Anna. She never put up with anyone's nonsense, including his. Everybody necessary to provide for his niece or nephew would be awaiting them. It would be just as it was when he was young.

Apollo stopped rocking the chair on Popi's porch. Was that what he wanted for the baby? A life like he had?

Crunch. Crunch.

The sound of footsteps on the crushed-seashell walk drew Apollo from his thoughts. It was dark out now. The reception had gone on for quite a while. And then there had been the toot of the ferryboat sweeping the guests off to the mainland.

The bright moonlight streaming down illuminated Popi's face. Apollo had to admit that if circumstances were different—way different—he would have been drawn to Popi. The fact that she was single and carrying someone else's baby didn't diminish the attraction.

The distinct intake of breath let him know that she'd spotted him, not that he'd been hiding.

Popi stomped up the couple of steps to the porch. She turned to him and pressed her hands to her hips. "What are you still doing here?"

He got to his feet. "I told you I wasn't leaving."

In the shadows, he wasn't able to see her clearly, but he got the distinct impression she was glaring at him. So be it. He wasn't here to make her happy—nor himself for that matter. He was here to make sure the right thing was done concerning the child. And that was for it be raised as a Drakos. He would teach them what they needed to know to take over the Drakos legacy, the way his brother would have done.

Toot-toot.

Another ferry was about to pull out with its load of happy but weary wedding guests. And that was just fine with him because he didn't want any other interruptions. He needed to get through to Popi that whatever she had planned for the baby wasn't going to happen.

She moved toward the door. "I'm tired. It's been a long day."

He moved in front of her. Having the entire evening alone, he'd formulated a plan. "I think you should move to Athens until the baby is born."

"Where I give birth is none of your concern. Now I'm going to bed. Good night, Mr. Drakos."

And without another word, she moved past him and entered the bungalow. The door slammed shut behind her.

When he'd arrived on the island, he hadn't known what to expect. It certainly hadn't been this very determined, very frustrating woman. But he could be just as stubborn.

He would not walk away from the baby—not like he walked away from his brother. He would be the man his brother wanted him to be. It was the least he could do.

CHAPTER SIX

HER BACK ACHED.

And it was getting worse the longer she lay there.

At least that's what Popi blamed her sleepless night on. She refused to admit that she couldn't stop thinking of Apollo. Each time she closed her eyes, she envisioned his blue gaze staring back at her. His eyes were spellbinding and totally unforgettable.

And then there was that toe-curling, spine-tingling kiss. Popi knew no matter how long she'd live, she would never forget that starry night in Apollo's arms.

She scrunched up her pillow and struggled to roll over, eager to find a more comfortable position. In the past week, there didn't seem to be any position that was comfortable for long. It wouldn't be too much longer until the baby arrived and she was able to get a good night's sleep.

In the meantime, with sleep being elusive, she played over the events of the evening. What was

Apollo doing here? There was nothing she'd heard about him that said he wanted to raise a baby. He couldn't even take time away from goofing off in order to attend his own brother's funeral. What sort of person did that?

Her arms moved protectively around her baby bump. This little one needed someone to adopt him or her that saw them as more than a Drakos heir. She could do that. She was uniquely qualified to be a loving adoptive parent—just like her adoptive parents had done for her and Andrina. They'd taken them both in at the tender ages of three and four and shown them that not all promises were broken. And most importantly that real love was in fact unconditional.

Could Apollo offer that to this child? Or would he be too worried about the position this child would hold in the Drakos dynasty? No matter his intentions, she would not be parted from this child of her heart.

Her sister and brother-in-law hadn't had the opportunity to make a will. Now it would be up to a judge—a total stranger—to decide the fate of this baby. She hoped and prayed they'd come to the right decision.

Was she scared of becoming a mother? Definitely. Did she have a clue what she was doing? Not at all. Just the thought of this little baby growing into a teenager with an attitude made her palms grow damp. But with love and a heaping dose of patience, they'd get through the growing pains. Popi had faith that all the good times, from the first words to the first steps to the first day of school, would greatly outweigh the challenges. That's what her parents had told her when she asked them how they put up with her through the teen years.

She would do her very best. It's the least she owed her sister...

Guilt welled up in her.

It felt wrong to be stepping into her sister's role as mother. Maybe if their last conversation hadn't gone so terribly wrong, Andrina would still be here. If Popi had been more understanding, maybe it would have made the difference between life and death.

But no matter how many times she went over the scenarios in her head, it wouldn't bring back her sister. Andrina was gone. And Popi had to pick up the pieces and move forward. No matter how difficult it could be at times.

Popi kicked off the sheet that was twisted around her legs. Using her arms to prop herself up in bed, she swung her feet over the edge of the mattress. She sat there for a moment. She never thought getting out of bed would be so much work.

She struggled to her feet, pressing a hand to the small of her back. She felt like she'd swallowed a beach ball. The baby agreed with a stomp of a

foot or punch of a hand on her bladder. Popi wad-
dled off to the bathroom for about the fourteenth
time that night.

After answering the call of nature, she didn't
feel like lying in bed and staring into the dark.
And standing made the discomfort in her back
ease a bit. Without turning on the lights, she
paced around the bungalow. She paused next to
the window.

She glanced out at the moonlight-drenched
sand beyond her small yard filled with lush foliage. She was so fortunate to live in paradise. But
even this beautiful land couldn't keep nightmares
from landing at her doorstep...

A movement in the corner of her eye caught
her attention. That was when she noticed an unusual shadow on the porch. It could be an animal.
But as she peered closer, she realized that it was
a person. The breath caught in her throat. Who
would be on her porch at this hour of the night?

Apollo?

Popi squinted harder into the night. Yep, it was
him. She let out the pent-up breath. He was sitting in the older rocker on her porch. His head
was tilted back and his arms were crossed over
his chest as he slept. He'd repurposed an old crate
that she'd turned into a plant stand and used it for
a footrest.

It was then that she realized by his waiting
for her to come home from the reception, where

she'd stayed late to oversee the cleanup, that he'd missed the last ferry to the mainland. And since the island was shut down for the pending renovations, there was nowhere for him to stay but with her. She sighed.

She should just turn away and let him be. After all, it was his choice to stay here. Just then the baby gave a hard kick that nearly doubled her over.

Rubbing her now sore side, Popi whispered, "Okay, little one. I hear you. He is your flesh and blood. As much as I want to pretend he doesn't exist, I won't kick him out of your life. He's the only one who can tell you about your father and his side of the family."

As an orphan who never knew her blood relatives, Popi knew the importance of family roots. She wouldn't deprive her child of that link—no matter how aggravating the uncle may be.

Popi grabbed a throw from the back of her couch that she hadn't had time to pack and moved to the door. Ever so quietly, she let herself out on the porch. She expected him to wake up at any moment, but he didn't stir. His breath was deep and even.

She tiptoed toward him and ever so gently draped the blanket over him. As soon as she had it over him, his breathing halted. He shifted positions as though getting more comfortable. Popi froze, knowing if she moved he'd wake up for sure. But then as quickly as his deep breathing had halted, it resumed, and so did Popi's.

She quietly tiptoed back inside the house. Tomorrow was going to be a very interesting day. Very interesting indeed.

Apollo jerked.

His eyes fluttered open just as his feet hit the floor. His heart pounded in his chest as he gulped down one breath of air after the other.

He glanced around, not knowing where he was. In the distance was the view of the sea. Slowly it all started to come back to him. The island. The baby. And the surrogate.

He was safe. He was on solid ground. And everything else had been a nightmare. Or more like a vivid memory. One that played over and over in his mind. It was one reason he'd considered giving up his nomad existence, but one tragedy had only led him to another much worse tragedy.

Apollo rubbed his thigh. The wound, though mostly healed, still bothered him at times, especially when he'd been on his feet a lot. And he was certain the dancing last night hadn't helped things. But he was a determined man. He had a lot to make up for and nothing was going to stop him.

It was only then that he noticed the blanket pooled around his waist. It took him a second to realize that Popi must have brought this out to him. So she knew he was still here and yet she hadn't woken him up to kick him off her property. Off the island. Interesting.

He would take that as a good sign—maybe she was starting to come to terms with the situation. With the sun barely above the horizon, he got to his feet and stretched. His stomach rumbled a complaint. He hadn't eaten since he was on the mainland yesterday.

The creak of the door announced Popi's presence. "You're still here?"

"Good morning," he said, hoping to get the day off to a good start.

He smiled at her as she stood there with no makeup on and her long hair pulled back in a loose ponytail. She looked so down-to-earth and approachable. He resisted the urge to move. As he continued to look at her, he noticed a glow about her. He'd heard it said that pregnant women get a glow about them, but he'd never known what that exactly meant, until now.

She didn't smile, but she didn't frown at him either. He'd take that as another good sign—something he could build on. Because the only way he was going to keep the unborn baby close was to keep Popi close.

"I started a pot of coffee. You might as well come inside. You can clean up and then have a cup."

She didn't have to invite him twice. He grabbed his backpack. After all these years, he didn't go anywhere without it. He followed her in the doorway. "Thank you."

After she handed him a towel, he grabbed a quick shower. The hot water beat on his sore neck, easing the painful kinks in his muscles. All too soon, he turned off the water. He didn't want to dally, as Popi seemed as though she might be in the mood to talk.

As he dried off and dressed in some fresh clothes, he hoped now that her shock over his sudden appearance on the island had subsided that she'd see him as something other than the enemy. He wanted to convince Popi to accompany him back to the Drakos estate, which was situated so much closer to a hospital.

Apollo entered the kitchen and inhaled the most delightful aroma. "The coffee smells wonderful."

"Help yourself. The cups are in the cabinet right above the coffeemaker."

He liked that she didn't stand on formalities and instead believed in a feel-at-home approach. He grabbed a cup and then glanced over his shoulder. "Can I get you a cup?"

She shook her head. "I can't have any. You know, being pregnant and all."

She'd made this pot of coffee just for him? It was just a simple act, but it got to him. It'd been quite a while since someone went out of their way for him. Usually when people figured out that he was "that Drakos," they wanted something from him—access to his brother, money to invest in some get-rich scheme and the list went on. But Popi didn't seem to want anything from him.

His gaze dipped to her baby bump. "I didn't know you couldn't drink coffee." And then he felt guilty. "I can dump it out."

Again, she shook her head. "Why should you go without? I'm the one that's pregnant. Pour yourself a cup and enjoy it for the both of us."

He arched a brow. She gestured for him to get on with it. And so he poured himself a cup. He'd learned a long time ago that milk was hard to come by out on the trail and sugar attracted all sorts of insects, so he'd learned to drink his coffee black.

The timer went off and Popi moved past him. She added eggs to the tomatoes simmering on the stove. As she continued to work in the kitchen, he moved to a stool at the small kitchen island, where he was out of her way.

"Whatever you're making, it smells good. Real good." His stomach rumbled in agreement.

"It's Peloponnesian scrambled eggs with fresh tomatoes and herbs. And it's almost done, if you'd like some."

"I'd love some."

Popi used a spatula to stir the contents of the pan. "My mother used to make them for me. But it's been a while. I don't get home to visit my parents as much as I'd like."

"Our housekeeper used to have these prepared for me on special mornings." He sent Popi a smile, hoping today would be a new start for them. "Looks like you're serving up a bit of nostalgia for both of us."

"I must admit that nothing I try makes the eggs as good as the ones from my childhood."

"I think sometimes our memories deceive us— makes the good things so much better than they truly were."

Popi lowered her gaze to the counter. "And the bad things?"

"I don't know." Because he tried to keep his bad memories locked up in the back of his mind. He didn't like to share them with anyone—including his late brother.

After adding some freshly chopped herbs and feta to the dish, she served it up. "Let's see how I did."

They ate quietly for a bit. He noticed that Popi was doing a good job at clearing her plate. He glanced down at his almost-full plate. The food was good but he was distracted by the change in Popi's mood. First the blanket and then being nice to him this morning. What was up with that?

He knew not to let his guard down because that's when people took advantage of you. It'd happened to him in the past—once by a vivacious blonde and another time by a fellow hiker that Apollo had come to think of as a close friend. Both turned out to be more interested in what he could do for them than being friends.

Is that what prompted Popi's change of mood toward him? Was she worried he'd take the heir to the Drakos fortune away from her? Because honestly, in the beginning, that had been his plan. He already had his team of attorneys working to quash her application for adoption. But now he wasn't sure that was the right approach. If they could handle this outside the courts, it'd be best for everyone.

Unable to take the curiosity any longer, Apollo asked, "Popi, why—"

Ring-ring. Ring-ring.

Popi held up a finger. "Hang on. I have to get this."

As she talked on the phone with more yeses and nos than anything else, he cleared the empty breakfast dishes. He stacked them in the sink as he would do if he were at home and there was a staff to finish cleaning up. But this wasn't his home. This was Popi's place. And this place didn't have a staff. There was just a very pregnant woman that for some reason was giving him a second chance.

Apollo picked up the first dish and started washing it. And the funny thing was he didn't mind. When he'd been off on his adventures, he'd learned to clean his own dishes, and in definitely more harsh terrain.

See, big brother, my travels weren't all a waste of time. I've learned to be a real human being and not just a spoiled brat.

The pain of loss engulfed him. It was so hard to believe that Nile was gone. He kept expecting him to walk through the door, slap him on the back and give him some verbal jab about his latest expedition. And then he'd tell Apollo all about his upcoming baby and how he was anxious to know him or her. Sadly, that was never to be—

"Sorry about that," Popi said, cutting through his painful and sorrowful thoughts. "That was the moving crew."

He placed the last of the dishes in the cupboard and turned to her. "That must be who you mistook me for yesterday."

She nodded. "Sorry about that." She got to her feet. "The ferry to the mainland will be here shortly. You can head down to the dock to wait for it." Popi started for the bedroom.

"Thank you for breakfast," he called out. "It was delicious and a nice reminder of the past."

Did she really think things were settled between them? Was that why she'd been so nice to him with the blanket and feeding him? Did she think he'd just quietly disappear?

He'd wait until she changed out of that flirty little pink robe and then they'd talk. He would tell her that there was no way he was giving away his own flesh and blood. And it doesn't matter how nice she is to him or how her smile lights up her eyes and causes a warm feeling within his chest. He was immune to her charms—if he wanted to be.

CHAPTER SEVEN

TOOT-TOOT.

The ferry was pulling into the dock. The work crew had arrived. It was time to get to work.

Popi tried to put socks on her feet, but her feet now seemed so far away. After a couple attempts, she tossed aside the socks. Flip-flops would have to suffice. Besides, with the swelling in her feet, she wasn't even sure she could get shoes on her feet.

She definitely didn't know about all of these discomforts when she'd signed on to be a surrogate. Not that it would have changed her mind. She would have done anything for her sister.

Like the time when they were young and her sister had strep throat. They were supposed to go with friends on a trip to the beach. They'd been waiting months to go and then Andrina had gotten sick. Popi could have gone without her big sister, but she knew how disappointed Andrina was about missing the trip. So Popi stayed home and they had a movie marathon instead. Their parents had promised them a trip to the beach when Andrina was better.

The memory brought a smile to her face, but it was fleeting, as the guilt over Andrina's death came back to her. Unlike when they were kids, Popi had let her sister down in the worst way. Popi never understood the true power of words until that moment.

And sometimes the lack of words was just as important.

The breakfast preparation had definitely paid off. There had been no arguing, and now Apollo was on his way to the dock and then on to the mainland. Oh, she had no doubt that their paths would cross again. And she also realized their attorneys would be hashing out the custody arrangement. But that didn't mean she had to deal with him one-on-one.

She pressed a hand to her lower back. With her stomach pushed so far to the front, it was really putting a strain on her back. And nothing she did would ease the pain. The only thing she could do was try to ignore it—like that was possible.

Popi changed into some work clothes, which was a challenge all its own. She was so far along now that barely any of her clothes fit comfortably.

When she at last slipped on some flip-flops, she headed for the door. Once she coordinated the transfer of everyone's belongings to the warehouses, she would be on her way to her parents' house. She was anxious to put her feet up and wait for this little one to make an appearance. In another couple of weeks, it'd be her due date.

Having her parents around would be a comfort. Her parents' home wasn't the place she'd originally envisioned waiting for the baby—that had been with her sister and her brother-in-law. It was amazing how fast life could change—with the flip of a coin. Her grieving parents were cheered with the prospect of becoming grandparents for the very first time.

Giving birth to this baby would be such bittersweet joy for all of them—

Someone cleared their throat.

Oh, no. Please say it isn't so.

Popi turned. There sat Apollo in the same chair that he'd slept in last night. That was it. That chair was going away. All it did was attract the riffraff.

"You better hurry," she said, trying to keep the agitation from her voice. "You don't want to miss the ferry…again."

Apollo got to his feet. "I'm not leaving. This—" he gestured between the two of them "—isn't finished."

"It is as far as I'm concerned. Our attorneys can handle it from here. Now I have work to do."

"Work?" A look of concern flickered over his face. "In your condition?"

"Yes, in my condition. I'm pregnant. Not dying."

"But still—"

"What did you think? That I'd lie around in bed all day and let the staff wait on me?" With dramatic flair, she pressed her fingertip to her chin. "Oh, wait. I don't have a staff. There's just me. And I do just fine on my own."

Without waiting for him to protest again, she turned and headed down the crushed-seashell walk. There was no way she was letting this man—this pushy guy—tell her what she could and couldn't do. It wasn't like she was planning to do any heavy lifting. She doubted she could bend over and right herself again without some help, much less bend down to pick up a piece of furniture. No, she already had a full load on board. She rubbed her belly, feeling a small bulge in the side, wondering if it was an elbow or a knee. Even the agitation of Apollo couldn't douse the smile the baby brought to her lips.

The crunch of seashells behind her let her know Apollo hadn't given up on his pursuit of her. Whatever. Let him waste his time. He could leave when the movers did—and that wouldn't be soon enough.

"Don't just walk away," Apollo called out. "I'm not letting this go."

She kept walking. "And I have work to do."

"Then I guess I'll help."

She sent him a warning glare. She had a lot to

coordinate today. She didn't need him getting in the way—

A sudden pain wrapped around from her back to the front. It knocked the air from her lungs. She stopped. She closed her eyes, for a moment blocking out the world—blocking out Apollo. But she could feel his presence lingering next to her.

"Popi, what's the matter?" Urgency and concern laced his words. "Is it the baby?"

She opened her eyes to find herself staring straight into his piercing blue gaze. Instead of it being disturbing or upsetting, she found herself comforted by his genuine concern.

And there was something more, but she couldn't quite name it. Or rather she didn't want to admit it, not even to herself. But her heart thump-thumped harder and faster. No man had a right to have such piercing blue eyes. It was as though they could see straight through her—see what she was hiding from the world.

But how could that be? She didn't even know him. And he certainly didn't know her. That's the way it must remain.

Because what she did know of him told her that he was the last person that she should count on. He was here today and gone the next. Never one to linger in any one place very long.

She shook her head. "The baby is fine. And so am I." Maybe it was a little white lie. She'd been pushing herself with the wedding and now the island renovation. After today, she promised herself that she'd rest until her due date. But for now, she had work to do. "I just need you to back off."

He held up his hands in surrender. "This is me backing off."

Without another word, she made her way past him, making sure their bodies didn't touch. There was just something about him—something that got to her. And she couldn't afford to let herself get distracted.

Something told her his definition of *backing off* and her definition of *backing off* were two different things. After all, this man came from great wealth, so he was used to getting what he wanted. But this time would be different.

A different approach was needed.

Pushing was not going to do it.

Apollo didn't know how he was going to get Popi to get off her feet and rest, but he was determined to do everything he could to make that happen as quickly as possible. And so he attempted not to say anything else to upset her.

He soon learned the plan was to clear the resident bungalows of their furnishings and the boxes so that tomorrow work crews could come in and give these older bungalows a makeover. Apollo wasn't sure exactly why this was being done for the whole island. All he was able to discern was that it had something to do with yesterday's wedding.

But he really didn't care about the island's makeover. All he cared about was Popi and the baby she was carrying. That acknowledgment struck him as he helped carry a couch out to the waiting trailer that would then haul everything to the warehouse.

This was the first time in Apollo's life where he had to put someone else's needs and well-being ahead of his own. He realized, at the age of thirty-two, that was a sad commentary on his life. But his father never needed or wanted anyone to fuss over him—Apollo wondered if his mother had been the exception. And his older brother, Nile, took care of Apollo, not the other way around.

As for his romantic relationships, well, after college they never got serious. He was never in one place long enough for any of that to take place—not that he would let it. "Once bitten and twice shy" was what they said. He said he was better off alone—that way he didn't fail to live up to other people's expectations and they didn't let him down.

As the work crew moved on down the lane to the next bungalow, Apollo turned, looking for Popi. She was nowhere in sight. Thinking that she'd gone on ahead, he returned to the bungalow to close the door.

He'd just pulled it closed when he heard, "Here, kitty, kitty. Come here, sweetie."

What in the world?

He moved to the side of the bungalow to find Popi down on her hands and knees. Her butt was sticking up at him. As she moved to look under a bush, her backside wiggled. For a moment, he was tongue-tied. He just watched—unable to take his eyes off her.

What was it about this woman that had him acting so out of character? Until now, he could take or leave female companionship. He kept to himself for the most part—communing with nature and its wonders. And the only time he cooked for others was when they shared a camp in the wilderness. When traveling together, it was common for everyone to take turns with the cooking.

But Popi was getting under his skin. And it was more than the baby she was carrying. And then there had been breakfast. Well, it had been nice—almost domestic. Not that he was thinking of settling into a life of domesticity or anything.

"Come on, kitty."

Popi's cajoling voice stirred him from his thoughts and released him from the trance she'd cast over him.

He stepped up next to her. "You shouldn't be down there. Let me help you up?"

Popi leaned back on her heels with a little gray kitten clutched to her chest. "Look who I found?"

"You have a cat?" He wasn't a cat person. Dogs, yes. Cats, no. Definitely not.

Cats couldn't go for walks or hiking or camping. When he was a kid, his friend had a cat. It was needy, pampered and wouldn't listen to a thing it was told. Apollo didn't need that in his life.

Popi shook her head, indicating that the cat was not hers. "It must have been left behind when all of the pets were moved to the mainland to be cared for until their owners returned from their cruise."

Apollo breathed a little easier. There were already so many distractions, so he didn't need more. As soon as he was done making sure Popi didn't overdo it today, they were going to revisit their prior talk and he was going to convince her that the best place for her and the baby was his family's home—the baby's future home.

He glanced down, finding Popi still sitting on the ground. "Give me your hand."

She appeared to be so distracted by the kitten clutched to her voluptuous chest that she did what he said without giving him a hard time about being able to do it herself. That was a first. Maybe if he was very lucky, it would be the start of something new between them. He could only hope.

"I need to get this little guy home," she said.

"But you don't know where he lives."

"Not his home. My home."

Apollo wasn't following her. "But you're moving out. You're leaving the island—"

"Not today."

"Of course you are. You have to."

Popi glowered, silencing him. "I've had a change of plans, which includes me staying until tomorrow."

"I'm confused." He rubbed a hand over the back of his head. He could feel the beginning of a headache coming on. "Why would you stay when everything is done?"

"Because I have to meet with the contractor tomorrow. Go over some last-minute details and hand over the keys." She sighed. "Not that it's any of your business."

She had a point. None of this was his problem. But that baby she was carrying, that was his responsibility. And like it or not, his feet were grounded to this island for the foreseeable future.

"I'd feel better if you were on the mainland, close to the doctor."

Popi made a note on her digital tablet. "I just had a checkup. Earlier this week. All is fine."

He pressed his hands to his sides. Why did she have to be so difficult? "It'd be safer if you were on the mainland—close to the hospital."

"You aren't going to let up, are you?" When he shook his head, she added, "Fine. I'll make you a deal. If you stop pestering me, I'll leave right away if anything seems worrisome."

It wasn't the answer he wanted, but it was better than nothing.

He nodded but didn't say what he was thinking. That pregnancy was dangerous—that his very own delivery had killed his mother. He didn't want history to repeat itself. It was one of the reasons he'd written off having a family of his own. He knew how devastating it could be when that dream fell apart.

But life had thrown him a twist. He was going to have a family—his brother's family. He just hoped he could be half the man his brother had been. The baby deserved nothing less.

Right now, the best thing he could do was to keep Popi off her feet as much as possible. In the morning, he'd get her back to the mainland—even if it meant he had to hire a helicopter to get them there.

He glanced at her as she fussed over the kitten. He had to admit he was a bit jealous of the kitten getting on Popi's good side, while she considered Apollo the enemy. But he was right about her going to the mainland. It was safest. But if she refused to listen to him, then perhaps he could get her to put up her feet and rest.

"Why don't you go back to the bungalow?" he suggested. When she sent him a suspicious look, he added, "You know, to take care of the kitten."

He'd also noticed that, as the day progressed, she'd been experiencing a lot of discomfort. He didn't know if that was normal at this point in her pregnancy. She consistently rubbed the small of her back. A time or two, she'd even let him give her a light massage, but the relief was always short-lived.

Popi's questioning gaze moved from him to the kitten and then back again. "I can't leave now. I have to make sure everything is put in the right spot in the warehouse and categorized accordingly. Can you imagine everyone returning to the island and not being able to find their belongings? Or worse, getting someone else's things?"

It seemed like with every moment that passed, he was getting sucked further into Popi's life. But she wasn't leaving him much choice. Someone had to make sure she took care of herself. And that obviously wasn't going to be her.

"You go back to the bungalow," he said. "I'll make sure the warehouse is taken care of."

She arched a brow. "Why would you do that?"

He stifled a sigh. Couldn't she just accept his help? Why did she have to question everything?

"Because you are tired. It's written all over your face." His gaze moved to the wiggling ball of fluff in her hands. "And because you aren't going to be able to hold on to the kitten much longer."

Just then she caught the kitten before it could climb the whole way up onto her shoulder. She settled it back in her arms. "Stay there," she said to the kitten as though it could understand her.

Then her gaze lifted to meet his. "And why should I trust you? I don't even know you."

"Our siblings were married, so that makes us family. Right?"

She hesitated. "Not really."

"Close enough. And if my brother were here—" just saying the words caused a large pang of hurt "—he would…he would vouch for me. I may not have been like him, but he understood that I had to follow my own path in life. Even if that path led away from him and our home."

Popi was quiet for a moment as her gaze searched his. "You really cared about him, didn't you?"

"Of course." He frowned at her. Why would she doubt such a thing? "Is that what my brother said? That I didn't care about him?"

She shook her head. "Forget it."

"Not a chance. I want to know why you would say such a thing."

She shrugged. "It's just that you were never there for the birthdays, the holidays. You weren't even there for their wedding or…"

She didn't have to say it. His mind filled in the blank. He wasn't there for the funeral. But he was here now. However, the look in Popi's eyes said that it was too little, too late.

Her gaze searched his. "You weren't interested in being part of the family then, so why the sudden interest now?"

Her words were like jagged rocks, beating against his chest. He hadn't meant to miss out on all of that. After each adventure, he told himself that he'd go on just one more excursion. He'd told himself that soon he would slow down. Soon there wouldn't be just one more mountain to conquer or one more adventure to go on. He'd always thought that there would be a tomorrow for him and his brother.

He of all people should have known that tomorrow is not guaranteed. The only thing you can count on is the here and now. That had to be enough. All the wishing in the world couldn't make the hands of time roll back. He knew this for a fact because it's what he'd been doing ever since he got the news of his brother's death.

He noticed the expectant look in Popi's eyes. She wanted him to argue with her. Well, she was in for a surprise.

"You're right." His voice was filled with remorse. "I wasn't there for those events, but I should have been. I was too wrapped up in my own life to realize what I was missing. I regret all of the missed opportunities."

She studied him for a moment, as though trying to discern the truth. "Do you really mean that?"

It was a sad commentary on him and his life when his devotion to his brother had to be questioned. "Growing up, Nile and I were close. I was the annoying little brother, but Nile put up with me. He took time out for me. When I wanted to quit college, he said that one day I would need to be able to run Drakos Industries. I just never thought it would be like this."

Popi glanced away. "I'm sorry. I shouldn't have doubted your relationship with your brother."

"It's not your fault. I've given you every reason to think I didn't care about Nile. I'll never forgive myself for losing track of what is truly important." He meant it. He had so many regrets that it was chewing him up on the inside. He wasn't about to add to that list. "I'm going to the warehouse now to make sure everything is completed. When I get back to the bungalow, we need to talk about the baby."

She handed over her digital tablet with all the necessary information about the furniture and boxes. "We can talk, but it's not going to change my mind about raising my niece."

"Or nephew."

She nodded. Without another word, she turned and did that really cute waddle thing. Eventually he caught himself standing there, staring as her. He gave his head a shake and then turned in the opposite direction.

CHAPTER EIGHT

THERE WERE DEFINITELY some benefits to being second-in-charge of the island.

Popi didn't feel that way most of the time. Most of the time being second-in-charge meant she had to run her ideas past Lea. It meant that any extravagances had to be preapproved by Lea. And sometimes being second-in-charge meant being the second place for a client to file a complaint, even if the situation was out of Popi's control.

But today Popi's position meant she could let herself into the small grocery store that carried so much more than food. She picked up some essentials for the kitten, from food to a litter box, and then she left an itemized list at the register of everything she'd taken. She would settle up when the island opened back up for business in a couple of months.

So much was about to change in the next six or seven weeks. Nothing would be as it had been. And her sister would not be there for any of it. And Popi blamed herself. If it wasn't for her making a fuss, her sister wouldn't have been on that boat when it exploded.

Popi shoved aside the guilt and pain. She had other matters to attend to now. There was the kitten locked up in her bathroom. And there was the sexy Greek man who insisted on staying in her life until he got his way. They'd see about that.

She wasn't just going to hand over this baby because he was a Drakos. Everyone in Athens—in Greece—knew his last name. They knew it was synonymous with old money and great power.

That wouldn't stop Popi from fighting for what was best for this child. Apollo might be the child's blood relation, but she was the one carrying the baby—making it possible for it to be here. And she wouldn't stop fighting for this little bundle of joy.

Once back at the bungalow, Popi was relieved to find that Apollo hadn't returned. But she didn't have time to rest. She had a kitten to care for.

In the bathroom, she was amazed to find that one little kitten could wreak such havoc. The toilet paper was strewn across the floor. Her purple-and-teal bath loofah that had been sitting on the edge of the tub was now across the room, and there was a kitten attached to it. The little guy was lying on his side while holding the loofah with its front paws and kicking it with his back. Popi could only hope that he wore himself out after making such a mess.

A little while later, the bathroom was set right and there was litter in the litter box. The kitten took right to the box. Popi could only hope that litter training was truly that easy and that there weren't any future accidents.

"Is everything okay?"

The sound of Apollo's voice made her jump. She hadn't heard him return. She turned in the hallway, finding him standing right behind her—so close that she could reach out and touch him. The thought was tempting—very tempting—but she resisted the urge.

"I didn't hear you come in," she said.

"Sorry. I didn't mean to startle you." He sent her a guilty grin.

When he wasn't frowning at her, he was really quite handsome. She wondered if the baby would resemble him in some way. She hoped so.

"Relax. I'm okay. I was just focused on the kitten." She frowned.

"What's wrong? Is it the baby? Did you overdo it today? I told you to rest earlier today, but you wouldn't listen."

"It's okay. It's not the baby. In fact, I think he or she is sleeping right now."

"Then why did you have that look on your face?"

"I was just thinking that I can't keep calling the kitten 'kitten.' It needs a name."

"And then you know what will happen, don't you?"

She sent him a puzzled look, not sure what he was getting at. "What will happen?"

"A cat with a name is a cat with a home."

She had to admit that she liked the idea. "Unless it already has a home."

"Something tells me that it isn't going anywhere." He was looking behind her.

She turned to see what he was staring at. There was the kitten dragging the loofah up to her. The kitten sat next to her.

"Looks like you have a shadow," Apollo teased.

"Shadow?" She looked at the dark gray kitten with the white neck and belly. She knelt down to pet the little guy. "What do you think? Are you a shadow?"

The kitten looked up at her with its pretty blue eyes and let out a little baby meow. Popi's heart swelled with love for it. Unless the owner showed up, it looked like she had a baby kitten to raise too.

Then she envisioned the baby with a kitten to grow up with. Somehow that seemed right to her. Now that she had her heart set on this vision of her family, she had to hope the kitten hadn't run away from a loving home and gotten left behind when everyone was shipped off the island for the renovations. And most of all, she had to pray that Apollo came to his senses and realized that the baby was best left here with her. Because if it came down to a court case, she had no doubt that he had the money to hire the very best army of lawyers and they would beat any defense she could muster.

Popi eyed Apollo, wondering if he'd really be that ruthless. There was a glint of determination in his eyes. Maybe she would have to mount her defense in a very different way—a way that didn't include lawyers and judges. She would have to appeal to his mind and his heart.

What was she thinking?

Apollo noticed the looks Popi had been giving him off and on all day. She had something on her mind, and he was pretty certain he wasn't going to like it.

It wasn't like she was just suddenly going to change her mind and hand over the baby when it was born. She had her mind made up about him, and he didn't know if he could change it.

When he was out in the wilderness, he didn't have to feel like he wasn't living up to other people's expectations of him. And he didn't have to feel like he didn't stack up to his big brother—the brother who had the perfect life, the perfect wife and the perfect career as CEO of Drakos Industries.

When Apollo was off on one of his adventures, the world became a lot smaller. He could focus on the more basic parts of life, such as his next meal and where he would sleep that night. Maybe that made him selfish—he wasn't sure. But at the time he'd gone off on his first adventure, he just couldn't stand to listen to one more of his father's lectures about how he was a disappointment. That was something Apollo would never say to his nephew or niece.

But he was starting to get similar looks from Popi—looks that said he'd let down his family and she would never trust him with the baby. The looks made him uncomfortable. After all, Popi barely even knew him. But she had heard stories from his brother. He could only guess at what his brother had to say about him, most likely none of it any good. In the last year or two, he and his brother had clashed—a lot.

Yet Popi still hadn't kicked him out. And he didn't miss the part about the village being deserted and it just being the two of them on the island. Did that mean he'd jumped to the wrong conclusions? Was it possible she trusted him? Just a little?

If so, it was a starting point from which he could reason with her and avoid a long, drawn-out, nasty court case that would be fodder for the headlines. The whole thing would be a mess.

"You really didn't have to stay here." Popi's voice drew him from his thoughts. "I'm fine on my own. And I have a phone should an emergency come up." Then she frowned as though realizing she'd said too much. "Not that there will be an emergency or anything."

He wasn't going anywhere. "I just feel better being here."

She arched a brow. "Are you saying you care?"

He suddenly felt as though there wasn't a right answer to her question. Not wanting to complicate things any further, he knew it was time to change the subject. "What would you like for dinner?"

A small smile pulled at her lips, letting him know she'd caught on to his diversionary tactics. "I don't know what's in the cabinets." She rubbed her back as a frown settled over her pretty face. "But I'm not hungry—"

Thunk. Thunk.

They both turned to the front door as it swung back and forth. The sun had set by then, leaving them in the dark. There wasn't even any moonlight tonight.

"The wind is really kicking up," Popi said. "I've been so busy with the wedding and packing that I haven't had time to check the weather in days."

She moved to the open front door. Another gust of wind rushed through the doorway. She pushed the door closed against the wind and secured it.

"Do you get bad weather here?" he asked.

"Once in a while. But not often."

Apollo started opening the kitchen cabinets. "It looks like we have pasta." He continued to name off the various food items. And then he turned to her. "What do you feel like?"

She rubbed the small of her back. "Um… nothing."

He moved to her. "Is your back still bothering you?"

She nodded. "I guess I overdid it today."

"You should be resting." He noticed the lines deepening between her brows.

She shook her head. "It'll pass. It always does."

Apollo expelled a long sigh. "I told you not to lift anything today."

"I didn't." When he arched a disbelieving brow at her, she amended her response. "Okay. But that box wasn't heavy at all. It had paper products in it."

"Maybe you were just on your feet too long." He glanced around the room for a place for her to sit, but they'd emptied most of this bungalow, as well as all the other bungalows on the island.

He scanned the now empty living room. He'd tried to convince her to keep some of the furniture, but Popi had been insistent that she could manage for one night with bare bones. He wondered if she was now regretting that decision.

He walked to the master bedroom to retrieve an inflatable mattress from the closet. He returned to the living room with it, some pillows and a blanket. He put them all down in the middle of the floor.

Popi was pacing back and forth. Her hand was still pressed to the small of her back. "What are you doing?"

"You need to rest and take some strain off your back."

"I'm fine."

"Don't take this the wrong way, but you don't look fine."

"Well, aren't you just full of compliments." She sent him a teasing smile.

"I try." At least she hadn't lost her sense of humor. They were going to need it to get through this night.

It took a bit to pump up the full-size mattress. Once he detached the pump, he fixed the mattress up with pillows and blankets. But what he hadn't counted on was trying to get a nine-month pregnant woman down to the floor. It took some maneuvering and cooperation, but at last Popi was off her feet.

She moved this way and that way, trying to get comfortable. And yet she continued to frown. She rolled onto her side and he placed a pillow behind her back.

"How's that?" he asked.

"It's good." But the look on her face said that it was anything but good.

He knelt down beside her. "We need to get you to the mainland."

He didn't like taking chances where her pregnancy was concerned. He knew what could happen. His family had already sustained so many losses. He didn't think he could bear another.

She smiled at him, but it didn't quite reach her eyes. "I'm good, really. You were right. I overdid it today. I should have listened to you."

Had she just admitted that he was right about something? He smiled. "You're sure?"

She nodded. "See. The pain is already lessening."

He studied her for a moment, trying to figure out if she was telling him the truth. There was no way they were staying on this island if she was going into labor. Not a chance. She needed to be in the hospital with a full, knowledgeable staff and equipment for any emergency. But in the end, even that hadn't been enough to save his mother.

Why exactly couldn't he have stayed gone for just a little longer? Just until the baby was born—when the beautiful surrogate mother and little one were safe and sound. He wasn't any good at this stuff. This waiting and wondering was taking its toll. But he didn't want Popi to see how worried he was.

"Maybe I should call your doctor." He straightened and reached for his phone. "Just to be sure."

"Don't." Her eyes pleaded with him. "I already ran to the doctor when I thought I was in premature labor last week. They assured me it was just Braxton-Hicks contractions."

"What's that?" He didn't like the sound of it.

"It's the body's way of preparing for the birth of the baby."

His gut was knotted up. "And you're sure that's what this is?"

She nodded. "We're good."

He still wasn't convinced that all was well. But what did he know about pregnant women? He could only trust that what Popi was saying was the truth.

His gaze searched hers. "You'll tell me if anything changes?"

"I will."

He released a pent-up breath. He needed something to do besides pace. "I suppose I should find us something to eat."

Just then Shadow emerged from whatever hiding spot he'd been cowering in since the winds started beating on the bungalow. The kitten let out a tiny cry, as though letting them know that he was hungry too.

"And I'll get you a bowl of kitten food." Apollo couldn't resist running his fingers over Shadow's downy-soft fur.

"And water. He keeps knocking his water bowl

over." Popi added just as the kitten climbed up on the mattress to be next to her.

Luckily Apollo had put down a couple of blankets to cover the mattress. Hopefully it'd protect it from the kitten's needlelike nails.

CHAPTER NINE

Could he trust her?

Apollo studied Popi while she fussed over the kitten. She was so stubborn and one determined lady. He worried she'd let these Braxton-Whatevers go too far. But she seemed all right for the moment.

Maybe she was right. Maybe there was nothing to worry about…for now. Besides, it wouldn't take long to get to the mainland by boat or helicopter.

One more pain and he didn't care what she said, he was calling for help. She was better safe than sorry.

In the meantime, he turned to the kitchen. Since Popi's newly remodeled kitchen wasn't being renovated, she hadn't felt the need to pack it up. That made it convenient for him. He set to work.

He needed to prepare a meal that was simple—something that was in his wheelhouse—yet it needed to be something with a bit of substance.

He settled for *fakés soúpa*. Popi had everything on hand, from the lentils to the onion and garlic. He warmed up a pot while he diced up the vegetables. It was a very easy recipe—

"What are you making?" Popi asked.

"Fakés soúpa." He added the chopped onion and minced garlic to the pot. "I hope that's all right."

"It's fine with me. So, tell me. Where did you learn to cook?"

"Here and there. It's a necessary skill when you're out on your own."

"And the soup? Was that something you made when you were hiking around the world?"

He glanced at her, finding genuine interest reflected in her eyes. "No. This is something I learned when I was a kid. When I would get in trouble with my father—which was most every day—Anna, our housekeeper, would either send me outside or if it was raining, she'd have me help in the kitchen."

"You and your father weren't close?"

He shook his head. "My father and I had a very strained relationship."

"I'm sorry to hear that."

"It's ancient history. But while I was in the kitchen, the cook told me that idle hands were the devil's workshop and so he put me to work. I actually didn't mind cooking. As it was, the cook and the housekeeper were the only ones besides my brother to have any one-on-one time with me."

"That sounds very lonely."

He shrugged. "I learned how to entertain myself and how to go it alone in life."

"And that's why you spend so much time off in some far-off jungle or climbing some mountain? It's all you've ever known."

She was right. But how had she done that? How had she read him so easily? He'd made it a point to close himself off to others. He'd built a wall around himself so no one would ever get close enough to hurt him again. And in such a short period of time, Popi had already scaled his wall and had a glimpse inside.

He cleared his throat. "I assure you the baby will never go through something like that. I'll make sure to give him—"

"Or her."

"Or her all the attention they need."

"You're still assuming the baby will be living with you."

It was time that she accepted reality. He placed the lid on the pot and let the soup simmer. He moved to the edge of the kitchen, where he could face her. He noticed how the kitten had curled up to Popi's chest and fallen asleep. She kept running a finger over its back. And when Apollo listened really hard, he could hear the kitten's purr. It sounded like the soft idling of a small engine.

"I'm waiting." Popi's voice drew him from his meandering thoughts.

His gaze met hers. "You have to realize that baby you're carrying, it's special. It's not your baby any more than it's mine. And it has a special place in life as the Drakos heir."

Popi's brows drew together. "Isn't that you?"

He shook his head. "My father wrote me out of the family business. He said I didn't have what it took to keep the company running. But Nile did. He was my father's favorite."

"But your father couldn't just cut you out of your inheritance—out of what is rightly yours."

"My father was powerful. No one told him what to do. He made up his own rules and expected everyone to follow them. He removed me from having anything to do with the company. While I was included in the will, it was my brother who inherited the controlling shares of the company."

"But with him gone, who's running it now?"

"At the moment, the board of trustees have stepped in to make sure there are no disruptions."

"And after that?"

"Well, since the baby is too young, there will be a conservator appointed."

"And that will be you?"

He shook his head and backed up. "It's not going to be me."

"Can't you do the job?"

"I could, if I wanted to. I might finally get

some use out of that expensive education that my brother convinced me to get. But I'm not going to do it."

"You're just going to turn your back on your legacy."

"That's where you're wrong. It's not my legacy. It never was." The memory of his father's harsh words came rushing back to him. *Worthless. Stupid. Mistake.* Each hurtful word was like a nail in his heart. How could those words still have such power to hurt him after all these years?

"Apollo—"

"No, I'm done talking about my past." His words came out more harshly than he'd intended. "We need to talk about the future. The baby needs to grow up in its home in Athens."

Popi glared at him. "You mean the same place where you were so obviously unhappy."

He sighed. She did have a point. "It will be different now. My father is no longer there."

"But will you be there? What about all of your adventures?"

That was something for him to consider. After being on the go for the past ten or so years, he couldn't imagine waking up in the same place day after day. Maybe when the baby got a bit older, he could take him...or her...on an adventure.

The outing would need to be more docile than he was used to taking. There would definitely be no thrill seeking, but something to get them out and about. He could teach the child about the world and how to care for it.

"I will deal with it."

Popi sent him an *I don't believe you* look. "Until you get bored."

"I won't get bored." Would he? He hoped not. But raising his nephew or niece would be such a different sort of lifestyle than he'd become accustomed to.

Before he'd only had himself to worry about. Now he'd have a tiny human counting on him for everything. The enormity of that responsibility did not elude him.

Popi sat up straighter. "You say that now, but things will change. Babies aren't always that easy to manage."

And just as she was talking him out of his plan, he recalled what his brother had done for him. "I understand that, but I also remember what my brother had sacrificed after our father died. He stepped up and became my legal guardian. He didn't have to do it. No one made him. But he said that family stuck together in good times and bad."

"I… I didn't know. Your brother never spoke about those times."

Apollo rubbed the back of his neck as the memories started to flood back to him. "It wasn't an easy time back then. There was a power grab for control of the company. They said my brother was too young and inexperienced to run such a large entity. And then the attorneys wanted me to go off to live with strangers. It was a horrible time. And I didn't make life any easier for my brother. I was full of anger. My brother was the undeserving recipient of a lot of hostility."

"It couldn't have been easy for either of you. You were both so young, and to lose both of your parents…"

"Even though everything was against us, my brother didn't give up. He fought tooth and nail to keep us together and to hold on to our father's legacy."

Outside, the winds continued to rage, beating upon the bungalow with force. Inside, Apollo's feelings were just as fierce. His emotions swung between remorse, love and guilt.

He didn't know why he was opening up to Popi like this. He'd never divulged any of this to another person. The only other person that knew of the struggles was his brother and he was no longer here to make Apollo feel connected to his family. That tie was gone and would soon be replaced by his brother's offspring.

"Your brother was an amazing man," Popi said, drawing Apollo from his thoughts.

"He definitely was." Those were words he was certain no one had ever spoken of him. You have to earn that sort of respect.

And before, that hadn't bothered him, but

now he wanted his nephew or niece to be able to look up to him. Not because he wanted the praise, but rather because he wanted to be that kind of person—the solid, dependable person that his brother had been for him. But was that even possible?

"And he loved you."

Apollo cleared the emotional knot in the back of his throat. "He tolerated me."

Popi shook her head. "It was much more than that. He stuck by you. No matter what. Even at his wedding, when someone would start to say something about you not attending, he would shut them down. He would tell them that you would be there if you could."

Apollo's head hung low as the weight on his heart grew more intense. "I should have been there." His voice was soft. "I wanted to be there."

A moment of silence passed.

"Why weren't you?" There was no tone of accusation to her question, but more a matter of wanting to understand.

Though they'd never met before now, they had shared a family. His brother, her sister. Popi had been there from the beginning of his brother's romance, through to the wedding and beyond… to offering to carry their baby. And Apollo had missed all of it. He'd chosen to isolate himself— to protect himself. Instead his plan had backfired. He'd hurt everyone, including himself.

"I had been in the Amazon rainforest. I had all my travel plans for the wedding, but then I was stung and came down with a bad case of dengue fever. I had some complications and it prevented me from traveling." But he should have pushed himself—he should have made it.

"I didn't know. Your brother didn't go into details."

"I'm sure that's because he was angry with me. And he had every right to be. When I needed him, he was always there. When he needed me, I failed him."

"But it wasn't your fault. It's not like you went out and sought out the illness. I'm sure you brother was disappointed but he understood."

"Really? Because I'm not sure I would be so understanding."

Just then the sky filled with light as a bolt of lightning shot through the inky night. Seconds passed and then thunder shook the bungalow, as well as them.

"I didn't know it was going to storm this bad," Popi said.

Apollo couldn't help but wonder if she was running out of words to comfort him and had decided it was best to change the subject. Before they let go of the past, he had one more thing to share with her.

His gaze met hers. "I've changed since the wedding. I've done a lot of growing up. I've witnessed a lot. I've had someone die in my arms. A good man. I've learned that we aren't guaranteed tomorrow and to make the most of today. I've learned to treasure those who care about you because there are many more that won't." When he saw the confusion in her eyes, he said, "What I'm trying to say is that I think I'm a better person now. I think—no, I know—that I can do this. Be a parent."

Another crack of thunder rattled the bungalow, making the glass of the windows rattle.

"I think we should check the forecast," Popi said.

He'd wanted her to acknowledge what he'd just said but then realized that she would probably disagree with him. After all, how could she not? He had missed his own brother's funeral. Who does that?

But he did have his reasons…

Popi struggled to stand up.

"Stay there," he said, seeing the lines of pain etched upon her face. "Your back—it isn't getting better, is it?"

She shook her head. "I think it's getting worse." She settled down on the mattress once again. "Why do these practice contractions have to happen now? Couldn't they have just waited a day or two?"

He couldn't tell if she was talking to him or herself. Regardless, he didn't think she was expecting a response. And so he remained silent.

"Could you hand me my laptop? I want to check the weather." She told him where he could locate it in her bedroom.

Once he returned to the sparse living room, he said, "I don't think you're going to need this. I have a strong feeling we're in for some rain tonight."

Just then the first drop of rain pinged off the window. And so the stormy night began. Apollo had this feeling deep in his gut that they were in trouble. And it wasn't like him to worry needlessly. After all, he was used to camping in jungles with wild animals, on top of mountains in the unforgiving snow and even lost in the desert during a sandstorm.

But there was one thing he'd learned from all of his experiences and that was to listen to his gut. He had some kind of crazy sense of imminent peril. But that's all it was—a feeling. It didn't come with any warnings of what to avoid or how to prepare. He just knew to be on guard.

While Popi used her computer, he moved to the front door. With the wind still blowing, he decided against opening the door. Instead he moved to the window. Even with the covered porch to protect the window from the now-pounding rain, he couldn't see more than a foot past the window. It was the blackest night he could remember.

He turned back to Popi. Her face was scrunched up in pain as her hand pressed to her rounded abdomen. The feeling of doom came over him again.

He rushed to her side. "Is there anything I can do?"

She shook her head as she let go of the laptop and leaned back against the pillows. "I don't understand it. The pain is getting worse. Usually it subsides by now."

And then he had the worst thought possible. He internally struggled with whether he should put voice to his thoughts. Saying it out loud and putting it into the universe was like tempting fate. But something told him that their fate had already been written.

CHAPTER TEN

APOLLO'S PULSE RACED.

He knew what was happening. Popi was going into labor.

In the next breath, he calmed himself with the knowledge that it was too early for labor. She'd told him earlier that day that she still had a couple of weeks until her due date. Everything was going to be all right. But he had to be sure.

"Could you be in labor?" he asked.

"Um. No. It'll stop."

That wasn't good enough. "We had a deal. I'm calling for the ferry."

"They won't come out this late. And certainly not to pick up the two of us."

"Then, a helicopter."

She shook her head. "It costs more money than I have."

"Don't worry about the money. We have to make sure you're okay."

Popi sighed. "There."

"What?"

"The pain, it subsided. Everything is going to be okay."

He didn't say it, but he didn't think they were in the clear. He thought this was just the calm before a stormy night. And he prayed he hadn't made the biggest mistake of their lives by letting her insist they remain on the island.

"You better check on the soup," she said, sending him a small smile. "I hear the lid rattling."

"How can you hear anything over the noise outside?"

As he moved to the kitchen to tend to the soup and adjust the temperature, he realized that he needed a plan. If the worst happened, he needed to get Popi to the hospital. Because she may be fine now, but she wasn't a few moments ago. And he was worried that it was going to happen again.

Flashes of his childhood raced through his mind. *It's your fault she died.* His father's drunken rants hadn't taunted him in many years. But these were extraordinary circumstances—a position he'd never wanted to find himself in. Ever. *If it wasn't for you, she'd still be here.*

"You're awfully quiet. Is everything okay?" Popi asked.

Apollo turned to find her getting to her feet. He rushed to her side to lend her a hand. "What are you doing? You're supposed to be resting."

"I feel better now. The pain in my back has

lessened. And I don't have any cramping. It's time to get the table set for dinner."

He stared at her. What had just happened? She'd been miserable and now she wanted to set the table for dinner? Was she really feeling that okay?

Not paying him the least bit of attention, she headed for the cabinets and retrieved two bowls. She moved without hesitation. And the little lines on her face had smoothed out. Maybe he'd just let his imagination get the best of him. After all, what guy wouldn't worry about being alone on an island with a pregnant woman—a very pregnant woman?

Lightning lit up the sky at the same time the power in the bungalow went out. Before either of them could speak, the lights flickered back on as a resounding clap of thunder shook everything. The storm was on top of them. And from the sounds of it outside, the island was definitely taking a hit.

He saw the worried look on Popi's face. "It's okay. It's just a little thunder."

She turned to the window. "It's not the thunder that worries me."

It was the lightning. It worried him too, as it was especially bad. But Popi didn't need anything else to worry about. "Don't worry. It should pass over in no time."

"Not soon enough."

He silently agreed.

The truth was that he couldn't wait until tomorrow. The contractor would arrive and they would leave the island. Soon they'd be part of civilization again—close to doctors, nurses and a state-of-the-art hospital. And maybe then he would be able to breathe easy. He didn't care how good she looked now—he still had that uneasy feeling in the pit of his stomach.

While he filled their bowls with steaming-hot soup, Popi paced the floor. Her hand pressed to the small of her back as though it were permanently attached there.

"Are you okay?" he asked.

"Um, sure. Fine." But those little lines returned to her face.

She wasn't fine—

The trickle of water caught both of their attention. They both glanced down to find a small puddle around Popi's feet. Either she just peed herself or they were in some *serious* trouble.

The breath stuck in his lungs as his gaze rose to meet her worried look. This was not good. Not good at all. He was freaking out on the inside but doing everything he could not to let it show. Like that was possible.

After all, he was a guy. He was used to traveling in the deepest, darkest jungles. He'd scaled rock walls. He'd lived through an avalanche. He

been attacked by a bear and had the scars to prove it.

But this baby stuff. It scared him silly.

"My water broke." Popi's voice wasn't much above a whisper. And the look in her round eyes was one of fear.

The two of them couldn't freak out at the same time. That much was for sure. And then he saw her eyes shimmer and a tear splash onto her cheek. Okay. She got the first turn at freaking out.

He told himself to pretend he was on one of his missions. Popi was just another adventurer. And his niece or nephew wasn't about to born. He also slammed the door on his past and stories of his birth. He just had to deal with the here and now.

He strode toward her. "You need to sit back down."

"Not like this. Not in these wet clothes."

In the next few minutes, Apollo did things that he'd never done before. And he did them in an almost out-of-body experience. He got Popi fresh clothes and, to both of their embarrassment, helped her change. Sometimes you just have to do what you have to do. And then he cleaned up the mess on the floor.

He'd never considered himself a squeamish person before, but then again, he'd never dealt with childbirth. And what little he'd been exposed to let him know it wasn't for the faint of heart. And it certainly wasn't for someone that didn't know what in the world he was doing.

Inside he was yelling: *Why did you do this? Why did you stay on this island when you could be near the hospital? Why would you take a chance with your life and the baby's?*

He strained, not letting his rolling emotions show on his face. It wouldn't help the situation. But it was tough to hold it all in when he knew what this early delivery could mean if they didn't get to the mainland soon.

"Go ahead and say it." Popi's voice drew him from his thoughts.

"Say what?"

"What you were thinking."

Had he let something slip? He didn't think so. "I'm not thinking anything."

"You're thinking this is all my fault." Her voice wavered. "You're thinking I made a mistake staying here. That I should have known better."

He avoided looking at her. He knew he should disagree with her. He should reassure her that none of this was her fault, but right now he couldn't.

He didn't think she'd used her best judgement by staying on the island. He thought she should have been close to the hospital throughout this whole pregnancy. Or maybe she shouldn't have gotten pregnant at all. Pregnancy was dangerous. It could take away those that loved you the most.

"Go ahead. Say it." Popi's voice rose with emotion.

"I don't have anything to say." Nothing that would help the situation.

"I just went to the doctor a few days ago." She blinked away unshed tears. "She said that everything was okay. She said that the baby was doing well. I thought—I thought wrong." Her shoulders hunched and her head hung low.

"That's good," he said, struggling to find something positive to say. "You know, that the doctor said everything is good with the baby."

Popi went on as though he hadn't even said anything. "I should have known the backache meant something. I should have known I was going into labor. If I can't figure out this stuff, how am I going to be a good mother?"

He couldn't just stand by and let her beat up on herself. Maybe he didn't agree with all of her choices, but he wasn't in her shoes. This island is her home. She would feel safe and secure here. That was a feeling he'd never experienced. His father's mansion had always been like a war zone when Apollo was growing up. And the worst part was he never knew when a verbal bomb would be lobbed in his direction. He banished thoughts of his past. He had to stay focused on the present.

The soup on the table was long forgotten. Apollo was running on autopilot. And his goal was to get them off this storm-ravaged island ASAP.

He reached for his phone. He started to dial for help but then noticed there were no bars. He had zero reception.

"Where's your phone?" he asked.

Popi grabbed it from the side of her bed and handed it to him. "What's wrong?"

He checked her phone too. "There's no cell signal."

"The storm must have taken out the tower."

The storm wasn't letting up. In fact, he'd swear it was getting worse, not better. But he wasn't about to tell Popi that. All she needed to do now was focus on that baby.

"There has to be another way to contact the mainland." He was certain of it. Okay. Maybe certain wasn't the right word. But he was desperate. It seemed reasonable that an island which hosted so many guests would have a backup plan.

"I don't know." Popi's eyes were open wide and her face was pale. "I… I can't think. The baby. It's coming."

A contraction stopped her from speaking. She began panting. He wondered if that was normal or not.

"Can I do anything?"

Right now, all he wanted to do was turn and

walk out that door. He didn't care if it was storming or not. It had to be better than watching Popi's beautiful face contort in pain. And he didn't even want to think about what lay ahead.

First, he had to do whatever he could to make her comfortable. He ran to the bedroom and grabbed any lingering throw pillows and blankets from the moving boxes. He propped all of the pillows against the wall and helped her settle back against it.

"What are we going to do?" Popi looked at him like he should have all the answers.

Meanwhile he was a wreck on the inside. He was just making stuff up as he went along and prayed that he was right. All the while reminding himself not to have a meltdown.

"We're going to get you off this island and to the mainland, where there will be help. Don't worry." Yeah, because he was worrying enough for the both of them. "This is all going to be okay. You and the baby will be fine."

The worry reflected in her eyes made the knot in his gut cinch tighter. He didn't believe what he was saying. He didn't believe this was going to be all right. There was no way he could do this alone. He had to get help and fast.

"Who is on this island besides us?"

"I... I don't know." She stared down at her protruding abdomen.

"Popi." When she didn't look at him, he placed a finger beneath her chin and lifted her head until her gaze met his. "Popi, think. Who is on the island?"

"Um, just some goat herders. Everyone else is off on a Mediterranean cruise for the next couple of weeks."

Apollo highly doubted goat herders would be any better at delivering a baby than him. So that idea was nixed. But he wasn't giving up. Their cell phones might not work, but there had to be another way to contact the mainland.

"Popi, what is the island's backup communication? You know, when the cell tower isn't working. How else can you reach help?"

Popi worried her lip as another contraction seized her focus. He took her hand in his, hoping to lend her whatever comfort he could offer. She squeezed his hand as her face scrunched up. The seconds seemed to last for minutes before the pain subsided. He couldn't even imagine what it must be like for Popi. If it were up to men to have the babies in this world, he'd been willing to bet there wouldn't be a population problem.

Once Popi relaxed, Apollo tried again. "Popi, think. How can I reach the mainland?"

"Um…" There was a moment of silence. "There are satellite phones on the boats."

That would work. He just had to make it

through the storm that was raging outside. "Great. You did awesome." He leaned over and kissed her forehead. "Don't worry. I'm going to get you out of here."

"Wait. What are you saying?" She clutched his hand tightly. "You aren't going to leave me here. Are you?"

"I have to." He really did hate leaving her alone. "But it won't be long. I promise."

"Please don't go."

Just then the kitten came bounding out of the bedroom. Without the thunder, the kitten must have decided it was safe to come out.

"Look," Apollo said, "Shadow is here. He'll keep you company."

Apollo grabbed a couple of small objects from the countertop, a paper flower from the wedding and a foam ball. "Do you mind if I let the kitten play with these?"

Popi shook her head.

It didn't take much to gain the kitten's attention. When it rolled over on its back, Apollo noticed the small smile pulling at Popi's lips. Thank goodness.

"Now, take care of Shadow while I'm gone."

"Take care how?" The worry returned to her eyes.

"Just play with him. And in no time, I'll be back." He lifted her hand to his lips and kissed it. "I promise. And I never break my promises."

And with that he headed for the door, having no idea what awaited him outside. But something told him it wouldn't be nearly as scary as what awaited him inside.

CHAPTER ELEVEN

PAIN UNLIKE ANY other gripped her.

Popi breathed through the contraction like she'd learned to do at her prenatal class. All the while, frantic thoughts raced through her mind. One worrisome thought proceeded the next.

Her sweaty palms rubbed over the blanket. Nothing about this delivery was right. It was too soon. She wasn't ready. Not even close. There was so much to do.

This wasn't how any of this was supposed to be. Her sister was supposed to be here by her side. This was supposed to be a joyous occasion. Not frightening and tinged with sadness.

The pain rose like a wave increasing with each heartbeat. And then it crested. It felt like it would go on forever. And then it rolled away, subsiding into nothing. At last Popi could breathe easily again.

She leaned back against the pillows and savored this pain-free moment. Maybe if she relaxed and didn't move, the contractions would stop. And then she remembered that her water had broken. There was no way out of this one. Birth was imminent.

But if it would slow down, that would be awesome. She needed off this island and quickly. Why did she insist on staying? Why?

She had to get it together for the baby. And for Apollo. He made a point of acting tough for her, but she could see in his eyes that he was afraid of this premature birth. He wasn't the only one.

This was her fault. She shouldn't have been lifting things yesterday. At the time, they hadn't been that heavy. She hadn't thought she was doing anything wrong. She'd just wanted to get the work over with so she could go home and rest.

She should have listened to Apollo when he'd told her to stop doing things. She should have gone to the mainland with everyone else. She should have been more prepared.

The regrets and—

Pain started again in her midsection, putting a halt to her rambling thoughts. The shortness between the contractions didn't escape her attention. She grabbed her phone so she could start timing them.

As the pain increased, she used the skills she'd learned from the midwife on the island and the prenatal class. She desperately tried to recall everything they'd told her. She just never thought she would be having the baby here.

She knew at nine minutes apart, she would still have some time before the baby. They needed all the time they could get to get off this island and to the hospital on the mainland.

She'd truly thought she would have more time before going into labor. This was her first baby and everyone had assured her that first babies were notoriously late. This baby apparently didn't want to be like everyone else, as it was coming a couple of weeks early—eager to put its stamp upon this world. And there was nothing and no one to stop it.

Now that the panic over the impending arrival of the baby was subsiding, she knew that she couldn't just lie here. The storm wasn't letting up—

Thunk!

Something heavy had hit the roof before rolling away. Popi glanced upward. She was relieved that there was no hole in the roof. The winds howled as greenery smacked the side of the bungalow. The storm wasn't letting up. In fact, it was getting worse.

With the tiny kitten cowering in her arms, she said, "Don't worry, Shadow. We'll be okay."

She had to get to the storm shutters on the windows and close them. The problem with that was they were on the outside of the bungalow. And she didn't relish the idea of heading out into the storm. But with Apollo already off trying to reach the mainland, that only left her.

She placed the kitten in a pile of blankets. "Stay there. I'll be back."

And so she struggled to her feet and headed for the door. It was pitch-black out. Definitely not a good sign. And the thought of Apollo being out there, alone, worried her.

He just had to be safe. She prayed he would return to her unharmed. She didn't know how she'd get through this without him.

He may have made mistakes in the past. And he may not have been there for his family when he should have been, but he wasn't the same man her sister had told her about.

The old Apollo—she could imagine him heading for the door at the first sign of trouble. He wouldn't have stayed with her, cooked for her and risked his life trying to get her help.

Maybe he wasn't exactly doing all of this for her, but he was doing it for the baby. At last he was learning that being part of a family meant being there for the good and the not-so-good.

Nile would be proud of his brother. She was proud of Apollo. She just wished he'd hurry back. With each passing minute, her worry escalated.

The fierce wind and rain stung his face.

The night was pitch-black.

Apollo squinted, trying to see where he was going. He stumbled over a tree root but somehow managed to stay upright. With the power outage, there were no lights to mark the path.

Apollo refused to be stopped. Walking against the fierce winds made each step a challenge. But in his mind's eye, he saw Popi's face contorted in pain and he remembered his father's mutterings that if they had gone to the hospital sooner, his mother might have lived. Apollo didn't know if that was true or not, but he also knew getting help as soon as possible was most definitely in everyone's best interest.

Thankfully he'd been down to the marina a number of times that day, hauling the overflow items that wouldn't fit in the island's warehouse. The extras were shipped to the mainland to be stored at another location. At the time, he hadn't been thrilled about taking trip after trip to the dock, but now he was grateful that he was able to draw on those memories to navigate his way in the dark.

It wasn't until he made it down to the marina that there was some light. He didn't know how. The rest of the island was cast in darkness. But down here, light reflected off the dock and the boats. There must be some sort of backup generator. Whatever it was, he was extremely grateful.

Because the storm had stirred the sea into a frenzy. The normally serene water now moved toward the island in swells, with white caps that crashed upon the shore. The anchored boats moved to and fro, straining against their moorings. It was a miracle they hadn't broken free.

The rain was now coming in sheets. He was soaked to the bone. And he was cold, but he brushed off his discomfort. This was the most important thing he'd done in his life. If he didn't get help, Popi and the baby might die.

That thought sent an additional flood of adrenaline rushing through his body. Once on the dock, he was left with the decision of how to get on a swiftly moving boat. And on top of it was the fact that the deck was wet. So even if he made the jump, who was to say that his feet wouldn't slip off the edge. His body tensed. It would not end well if he were caught between the boat and dock.

Once he decided upon a boat, he studied it. In. Out. In. Out.

At least the boat appeared to be moving at a predictable speed. Before he could talk himself out of this, he jumped. Grabbing a rail and holding on for his life. For a moment, he didn't move, as he struggled to gain his footing.

And then he moved cautiously from the stern of the small yacht toward the bow. It was easy enough for him to find the control room. He wiped the rain from his face before swiping his dripping wet hair back, out of the way.

Once he turned the lights on, he went to work. With all of the adventures he'd experienced over the years, boating hadn't been one of them. He'd just never gotten to it. When it came to his excursions, he'd always favored the kind where he was physically challenged. When he thought of boating, he thought of lazy days on the deck, enjoying the sunshine. Obviously there was more to boating than he'd first assumed.

A strong current struck the boat. Apollo lost his balance. His shoulder hit the corner of a cabinet. That was going to hurt in the morning.

All he knew now was that he had to radio for help because there was no way he could deliver a baby. He didn't know the first thing about childbirth.

Another wave struck the boat, sending him stumbling to the floor. He didn't have much time before this yacht broke free of the dock. And there wasn't anything he wouldn't do to make sure Popi and the baby were safe.

CHAPTER TWELVE

THE BUNGALOW WAS SECURED.

But Apollo hadn't returned.

With every passing minute, Popi's concern for him mounted. She should have insisted he stay here. It wasn't fit for man or beast out there. But it wasn't like he would listen to her. It hadn't taken her very long to deduce that he was a stubborn man.

The door flung open. Apollo stepped inside. Wind rushed into the room, sending the kitten scurrying away. With effort, Apollo closed the door, shutting out the storm. He kicked off his wet shoes.

He was drenched with rivulets of rain racing down his face. She tossed him a towel that she'd used earlier to wipe off after venturing outside. He swiped it over his face before running it over his hair.

Holding the towel to his chest, his gaze turned to her. "How are you?"

She pressed a hand to her rounded abdomen. "Still pregnant."

"And the contractions? Did they stop?"

She shook her head. "They're coming at seven minutes apart."

"What does that mean?"

She shrugged. "I think there's still time to get to the hospital if this storm would let up." Now it was time for her to ask a question. "Were you able to reach anyone?"

He nodded but his gaze didn't quite meet hers. "I did—"

"You did? That's great!" But the look on his face said otherwise. "When will they be here?"

"They won't be."

"What? But why?"

"The storm is a lot worse than we thought. They can't get to us via sea or air until this storm is over."

"Oh." Another contraction stole her voice away.

Apollo rushed to her side. He grunted in pain as he knelt down next to her, but she couldn't ask him about it—not yet. He took her hand in his. His hand was dry but his skin was cold to the touch. The wave of pain rose...rose...and crested. And then it was slow to ebb away.

When the pain fully passed, she sighed. "I can't believe the pain is going to get worse. This feels plenty bad right now."

"Don't think about it. You're doing great."

"I sure don't feel like it."

He gave her hand a quick squeeze before he released it. As he went to straighten, she noticed his cargo shorts had risen up slightly on his muscular thighs. That was when she noticed a long scar starting near his knee and snaking up under his clothes. It was still pink, as though the scar were recent.

Once fully upright, he said, "I'll be right back. I need to get out of these clothes." He turned toward the bedroom but then paused and turned back. "Do you need anything first?"

She shook her head. "I'm good. Thanks."

The truth was she had a lot of questions for him. She wanted to know when this storm was going to move on. She wanted to know if he got any other information from the mainland. And she wanted to know about the scar on his leg. Did it have something to do with why he'd missed his own brother's funeral?

Seconds ticked away as Popi flipped through her pregnancy book, gleaning any information that would help them. She wondered if there was any way to delay this delivery until help reached them. She didn't recall reading anything like that, but maybe she missed it. Originally she'd been planning to stay with her sister in the city. And when that plan had fallen through, she'd made the backup plan to stay with her parents. At this point, they didn't even know that she was in labor, and she had no way of telling them.

Apollo entered the room again. His gaze moved to the kitchen island. "You didn't want to eat?"

She shook her head. "I didn't think it was a good idea under the circumstances."

He nodded in understanding.

"You can go ahead and eat," she said. "In fact, I insist."

"That's okay."

But she knew it wasn't. He had to be starving, especially with his hike to the marina. "Please eat. You don't know how long we're going to be here."

His hesitant gaze moved between her and the food.

"Go ahead," she said.

His worried gaze turned back to her. "Shouldn't you eat something too?"

She shook her head. "I'm good."

He moved to the counter. "You know I feel really guilty about eating when you aren't."

That touched her. "Tell you what, after this baby is born, I'm going to be starved. You can feed me then." She thought it would make him feel better, but instead the worry reflected in his eyes was now written all over his face.

"You bet." His voice lacked enthusiasm. "Anything you want."

Another contraction stole her voice. She sucked in her breath, holding it. She leaned forward and squeezed her eyes closed as the pain increased. She willed the pain to go away, but it seemed like the pain grew in strength and length as her labor progressed. Would she be able to hold out until help reached them?

The next thing she knew, there were hands on her back. She opened her eyes in surprise to find Apollo kneeling next to her. His big hands and long fingers gently kneaded her back.

"Breath in," he reminded her. His voice was deep and soothing.

She did as he said.

"And breath out." All the while, his hands moved over her aching back. "Now again." He breathed with her as though they were in this together.

After a while, the pain slowly ebbed away. She leaned back on the mound of pillows. "How did you know how to do that?"

"I did a little research while I waited for you to return from the wedding. I had a lot of time to kill and knew nothing about pregnancy. I wanted some idea of what to expect."

She looked at Apollo with a new kind of appreciation. There was definitely more to this man that anyone ever gave him credit for. She wondered what else there was to him. Because the more time she spent with him, the more curious she became.

"So, tell me about yourself," she said.

He shook his head. "There's not much to say."

"Really? I'd think there would be quite a lot to tell."

"I'm sure it's nothing you'd be interested in."

Why was he so insistent on putting her off? He was an adventurer. He'd been to more places on earth than she could ever imagine going. She would have thought he would be full of stories—of conquests. She would imagine him at pubs, entertaining the men and women with his brave and daring feats.

And needing something to concentrate on besides the inevitable next wave of pain and whether help would reach them before this baby decided to make its appearance, she had to get him talking. Besides, if they were to co-parent, she wanted to know exactly what sort of man she was getting involved with—in a purely platonic sort of way. Though the thought of something more between them was certainly very tempting—even if it was completely out of the question.

She patted a spot on the mattress next to her. "Come sit beside me."

"I don't think that's a good idea."

"Why not? It's not like there are a lot of other seats around here, with the furniture already moved to the warehouse."

His hesitant gaze moved from her to the spot next to her. Still, he made no motion to move. "Maybe I should—"

"Entertain me." When he sent her a puzzled

look, she said, "I'm serious. Come talk to me so I don't sit here and think about how soon the next contraction will hit me."

Still, he didn't move.

"Please." She pleaded with her eyes. "After all, I'm doing all of the hard work here."

That seemed to have done it. The next thing she knew, the mattress dipped as he lowered himself next to her. It wasn't until then that she realized just how small the mattress was. Apollo's thigh brushed up against hers, sending her heart aflutter. Which was totally insane, considering she was getting ready to give birth. But she was beginning to think there wasn't anything that could keep her from noticing Apollo and his sexiness.

She swallowed hard. "So, um, tell me about one of your adventures."

"Is that really what you want to talk about?"

She nodded, not trusting her voice.

"I've visited the Amazon rainforest. I was there for a few months."

"Months?" When he nodded in confirmation, she asked, "You mean out in the jungle, with all of those insects and snakes?" Her nose curled up at the thought of pitching a tent and having some creepy-crawly come curl up with her.

Apollo let out a soft rumble of laughter.

Her gaze met his, and it was then that she realized just how close he was. He was so close that it would be nothing for her to lean over and press her lips to his. Her gaze momentarily dipped to his mouth. She remembered just how skilled he was at kissing. And as tempting as the thought was, now was certainly not the time. There wasn't a chance he could find her attractive as he ran a cloth across her forehead. He'd probably never find her attractive again. She smothered a sigh.

"Popi?" His voice startled her from her rousing thoughts.

And it came just as another contraction ruined this perfectly nice moment. She turned away and ground her back teeth together. The breath hitched in her throat as she braced for the pain to reach its peak.

Apollo took her hand in his. His thumb stroked gently over the back of her hand. "Remember to breathe through the pain." His voice was gentle. "That's it. In. And out. In. And out."

And then he did the breathing with her. It touched her heart that he was trying so hard to be there for her. Neither one of them were sure exactly what they were doing. And as this pain was worse than the last, she knew the chance of the storm letting up and allowing help to reach them before this baby made its grand entrance was slipping away with each passing contraction.

"You're doing great." Apollo continued to hold her hand.

As the pain neared its strongest point, she squeezed his hand. Tight. Very tight. He didn't say anything. Nor did he try to pull away. And though in the beginning she hadn't wanted him here for any of this, she now found comfort in his quiet strength and took solace in his encouraging words.

But she wasn't sure either of them was up for all of this. If this was how bad the pain was now, how much worse was it to get when the baby was finally born? The thought sent an arrow of fear through her.

She couldn't do this. She never should have agreed to have this baby for her sister. Sure, women had babies all the time, but they were different than her—they were braver and stronger.

As the pain ebbed away, she said, "I don't know if I can do this."

Apollo placed a finger beneath her chin and turned her head until their gazes met. "You can do this. You are doing amazing so far. I've never seen anyone as brave as you."

She didn't believe him. "You're wrong." Panic clawed at her. "I can't do this."

"I swear you are the bravest."

"But you've done all kinds of brave things, from hiking and camping in the jungle to mountain climbing. I'm just having a baby."

"Having a baby is one of the bravest things a person can do. And climbing a mountain doesn't even compare." His voice faded away, as though he were lost in his thoughts.

She was supposed to have another couple of weeks before all of this. Even her doctor hadn't said anything about her going into preterm labor. If she was going to be a parent, she had to do better—be more prepared.

"Popi, I'm in awe of you."

He was? Had she heard him correctly? He was in awe of her?

She turned to him and found warmth reflected in his eyes. "You really mean that, don't you?"

"I do. This little baby is going to have the most amazing mother."

What did that mean? Was he telling her that he was going to relinquish his quest to have custody of the baby?

She never got to ask the question, as another more powerful contraction swept her breath away. She held on tight to Apollo's hand as she rode the painful wave.

CHAPTER THIRTEEN

WHAT EXACTLY HAD he gotten himself into?

Time passed slowly. Very slowly.

Apollo sat by helplessly as Popi writhed in pain. It was more horrible than even he had ever imagined, not that he thought about childbirth much. In fact, he'd spent his whole life avoiding the subject. But he hadn't been able to avoid the guilt that shrouded his youth over him surviving while his mother had not.

But that wasn't going to happen with Popi. She would make it. The medevac would be here shortly. He was positive of it. Because there was no way he was delivering that baby.

As more time passed, Popi's contractions were a mere two minutes apart. The winds and rain continued to pummel the bungalow. His hopes of a quick rescue were slipping away.

It was going to be up to him to make sure Popi held the baby in her arms at the end of all of this. That seemed like a very daunting task.

"Talk to me." Popi's voice drew him out of his thoughts.

"What do you want me to talk about?"

She pulled her hand from his and ran her finger along the uneven scar trailing down his thigh, where his shorts had ridden up. "Tell me about that."

"You don't want to hear about it."

"I do. Please tell me. Give me something to concentrate on besides the contractions."

With all she was going through to bring a healthy baby into this world, he had no right to withhold her one request. But where did he begin?

He cleared his throat. "I was on an extended trip in the Himalayas when it happened."

"What were you doing there?"

He shrugged. "Would you believe me if I told you that I threw a dart at a map and that's where it landed?"

She looked at him with disbelief reflected in her eyes. "Are you serious?"

"Pretty much. The dart method has taken me to some of the most interesting places on this earth. Some places I'd rather have not visited. This was one of those places."

"You mean because you got hurt?"

Just then her hand sought out his, and he knew what was coming—another contraction. He couldn't believe the contractions just kept coming one right after the other. It was well into the middle of the night by now. And lines of exhaustion were written on Popi's face.

"Keep talking," she said before groaning in pain.

And so he did as she asked. "I spoke to Nile before I went on the trip. I wanted him to know that I'd be completely out of touch for a couple of months. Nile told me about the baby and wanted me to be available in case there was any news about the baby. In fact, he demanded I forgo the trip and pick up the slack at the office so he could spend more time at home." Apollo paused and wiped the sweat from her brow, never once letting go of her hand. "I didn't know it at the time, but it would be the last thing that he ever asked of me. So we ended up arguing." Apollo expelled a sigh. "If I had known—if I'd had any clue that was to be my last conversation with him, it would have ended so differently."

"I'm sure Nile knew how much you cared about him."

"Really? Because the last thing I told him was to butt out of my life. He wasn't my father and he couldn't boss me around."

Apollo could tell Popi's pain was lessening, as her grip on his hand loosened. He didn't think that his hand would ever be the same after this night. If he made it through without any broken bones, he would count himself as lucky. But right now, that would be a small sacrifice compared to what Popi was going through.

"You couldn't have known it would be your last conversation. None of us knew what was going to happen."

"But my brother didn't ask much of me. For years, he just let me be to chase one adventure after another, like some overgrown kid. And the one time he needed me, I'm too busy for him."

"He wanted you to be happy. He knew you'd had an unhappy childhood."

"It's something I never want this baby to go through." His gaze met hers. "I want us to figure out a way for the child to be happy."

"We will." She gave his hand a quick squeeze. "But what happened on the hike?"

"There was an earthquake. The ground beneath my feet literally disappeared. And that is the last thing I remember."

"That's horrible." Her gaze moved back to his leg.

"They say I fell, tumbled, rolled—you get the idea—about two hundred to three hundred meters. I ended up buried in rocks. Luckily I wasn't alone on the hike. Others were more fortunate than me. They called for help and dug me out."

The color drained from Popi's face.

He knew this wasn't the story to tell her—especially now. If only she hadn't insisted. "I was unconscious when they found me. I'm told I had a broken leg, fractured ribs and a collapsed lung."

Popi gasped. "You're lucky to be alive."

He nodded. "For a while, I wondered why I'd been spared while others hadn't. Now I guess I have my answer." His gaze moved to her baby bump. "But it shouldn't be me here. It should be my brother. What kind of mixed-up fate is this?"

The pressure on his hand tightened. Another contraction was building. While Popi panted her way through it, he kept talking.

"While I was in the hospital, I'd slipped into a coma. Apparently the hard head I've been accused of having isn't much of a challenge to rocks."

Another contraction commenced. He wasn't sure Popi could hear him at this point, but he kept talking just like she'd asked. "I was in a coma when they died. It's why I didn't make it to the funeral. I remember dreaming of Niles. You know, while I was in a coma. I don't remember anything else, just seeing him and talking to him. He was as real to me as you are."

He recalled how Nile had said that he was proud of Apollo. They'd walked and talked like... like brothers.

"Do you think it was your brother saying goodbye?"

Apollo didn't say anything at first as he pondered the question. He wasn't sure what he believed about the hereafter. Did he think the dead could speak? No. He certainly didn't believe in ghosts.

As though Popi were privy to his internal debate, she said, "You know you were in a coma at the same time as…as the accident."

He knew what she'd meant to say—he was in a coma at the same time that his brother had died. Was it possible that it was truly Nile speaking to him in his dreams? Would Nile really have said that he loved and forgave Apollo? He wanted to believe it, but he knew it had just been wishful thinking on his part.

Not wanting to think about it any longer, Apollo steered the conversation away from the ghost of his brother. "I never thanked you for making all of the funeral arrangements. You don't know how bad I felt when I woke up in the hospital and found out that I had lived while my brother had died."

"That must have been horrible." Popi leaned her head against his shoulder. "I'm sorry."

Not being there for his brother and cutting Nile most of the way out of his life—they were the regrets that weighed upon his heart. He wasn't sure he would ever forgive himself for living while his brother died without ever getting to meet his little son or daughter.

Though Apollo did find comfort in Popi's words, he didn't feel he deserved them. "You have nothing to be sorry about. You lost just as much as I did that day."

Popi didn't say anything. He felt her body grow rigid. And then her grip on his hand tightened once more. The baby was almost here.

His gaze moved to the window. It was still dark out. But as he listened, he noticed that the turbulence of the storm had dissipated. But would help be able to reach them before the baby arrived?

"I need to push," Popi said between pants.

His blood ran cold with the thought of being responsible for the lives of Popi and the baby. His mother hadn't survived childbirth, and she'd been in the hospital, with people who knew what they were doing. He didn't have a clue besides what he'd read, and that hadn't been much.

Please let them be okay. Please.

CHAPTER FOURTEEN

"WAAH... WAAH... WAAH..."

Popi used her last bit of energy to smile.

They'd done it. Together they'd brought a new life into the world. And it was amazing. It was miraculous. And she'd never known such happiness.

"It's a boy." Apollo placed the baby, wrapped in a soft towel, on her chest.

Popi glanced up at her hero and noticed how pale he looked. In fact, he looked as though he were about to pass out.

"You should sit down." She attempted to move over, but her body protested the thought of moving so soon.

"Maybe I will." Apollo sunk down on the floor. He didn't seem to care that there was no mattress beneath him. He drew his knees up and rested his arms on them. He glanced over at her. "You were amazing."

"We were amazing." She turned to the baby in her arms, who'd calmed down now. "But you are the star of the day."

Apollo leaned in close. His finger stroked the baby's cheek. "You are a miracle, little guy."

"I just wish..."

She didn't have to say it, because he'd felt the same way. "I wish the same thing. His parents would be so proud of him."

A tear rushed down Popi's cheek. "They definitely would."

Whup. Whup. Whup.

The sound of an approaching helicopter gave Apollo his second wind. In a heartbeat, he was on his feet. He rushed to the door and swung it wide open.

He stepped out onto the porch. The early morning sun was shining brightly as a gentle breeze circulated through the bungalow.

"How is it out there?" she asked.

"Blue skies and a calm sea."

"What about the island?"

"It's nothing for you to worry about."

Which is exactly what it did—worry her. If it was so bad that he wouldn't even tell her the damage, it must be really bad. Thank goodness they had a crew showing up today. It would appear they had more work ahead of them than they'd originally been planning on. She just hoped they were up for the challenge. Because she wasn't. She had other priorities now.

She turned her attention to the cutest little boy in her arms. He had blue eyes that seemed to take in everything around him. And a head full of dark hair. He was definitely going to be a heartbreaker when he grew up—just like his uncle.

Just then Shadow decided to make an appearance after hiding for most of the night. He crept forward, stretching his neck out and sniffing the new baby. Popi smiled. Something told her that these two were going to be good friends.

As for her and Apollo, she didn't know how things were going to work out now that they were about to leave the island. But their time on the island had most definitely changed things between them. The Apollo that she thought she'd known was much different than the actual caring, giving man that was now crouching next to her to fuss over the baby.

But even though she'd come to know this caring and gentle side of him, she knew that he still had an adventurous side. Would that mean he would leave the baby with her?

There were still so many unanswered questions. But as the paramedics made their way inside the bungalow, she knew any answers would have to wait until much later.

CHAPTER FIFTEEN

HOME FROM THE HOSPITAL.

Home. The word felt so strange.

Apollo opened one of the ominous oversize black doors with bronze fixtures. The Drakos estate had staff to open doors and such, but he'd been fending for himself for so long that he was no longer used to being fussed over. He knew that would change by moving back into this gigantic mausoleum of memories.

He hadn't alerted any of the staff of his exact arrival. He'd wanted his return to be low-key. He wasn't sure how he would feel first walking in here. While Popi had been in the hospital, he'd stayed in a hotel close by, not wanting to be far from her or the baby should they need him. And perhaps a tiny part of him had been relieved to have a legitimate reason to put off his return.

He glanced around the grand foyer with its gleaming marble floors. He recalled as a boy running into the room in his socks and sliding across the floor. His gaze moved to the grand staircase, where his father used to stand at the top with a glass of bourbon in one hand, while with the other hand he'd point an accusing finger at Apollo for one offense or another.

He recalled one specific instance when his father had stood at the top of the steps and glared down at Apollo like he was master of the universe. Apollo would get blamed for misdeeds he'd done and sometimes for misdeeds that were not his. And as he grew older, his attitude toward his father became more hostile.

There was a specific day when his father had blamed him for something that was clearly not his fault and called him worthless, and Apollo had shouted that he hated his father. His outburst had been rewarded with his father raising his hand and launching his still-full glass of bourbon down the steps at Apollo. The vivid memory caused Apollo to flinch.

Popi's hand touched his shoulder. "Are you okay?"

He glanced down at the marble floor, where he'd been standing that day. If he hadn't moved, the glass would have hit him. He choked down the lump in the back of his throat. But when he spoke, his voice had a hoarseness. "I'm fine."

Looking back now, he wondered if that was the day his father wrote him out of the family business, or had that already been a forgone conclusion from the tragic day when he was born? Not that it mattered to him. He could take or leave the business world.

He'd learned a lot about the world and himself when he'd been off on his adventures. He was no longer the kid filled with rage over his crappy childhood, where he'd never known his mother, and his father had said one abusive comment after the next.

He shoved the dark memories to the back of his mind. Things would be different for the baby. Apollo would make sure their precious little boy never had to run from hateful words or flying glasses. The only time he would run from Apollo was when he was threatening to tickle his nephew.

Apollo turned to Popi, who was holding the sleeping baby in her arms. "Let's get you and the little guy situated."

"Thank you for letting us stay here while my parents are recovering from the flu."

"Not a problem." In truth, it had all worked out the way he'd wanted. He just didn't realize after all these years that this place would still get to him.

Just then Anna, the housekeeper, entered the foyer. Her face lit up with a big smile that made her warm eyes twinkle with genuine happiness. "Mister Drakos, you're home. It's been too long."

"Hello, Anna."

It was then that she broke with protocol and gave him a hug. It wasn't the first time, nor would it be the last, that she bent the rules that had governed the Drakos estate for as long as Apollo could remember. Maybe that's what the place needed—a break with the routine of the past.

He hugged her back. She was the closest thing that he'd ever had for a mother. And it was only now that he realized how relieved he was that she was still here for him to come home to. Between Popi, the baby and Anna, he would do his best to make peace with living here amongst the ghosts.

Anna pulled back and turned to Popi. "And who do we have here?"

She knew because Apollo had called ahead to make sure the house was spiffed up and a room had been set up for Popi and the baby. But he knew that Anna was fishing for an introduction.

"Popi, I'd like you to meet Anna. She is the housekeeper, but in truth she's the one that keeps this house functioning. Without her, the place would fall apart."

Anna's cheeks took on a pink hue, but she didn't say anything.

"It's so nice to meet you." Popi smiled.

"If you need anything at all," Anna said, "just let me know." And then she stepped closer. "May I see him?"

Popi pulled the blanket away from the baby's face to give Anna a good look at him. "Would you like to hold him?"

Anna's eyes widened and her face filled with excitement. "I would."

Apollo watched as the two women interacted with ease. He breathed a little easier. This would definitely help with his ultimate plan—getting Popi to agree to stay here with him and the baby.

One day passed into the next in what felt like a five-star hotel.

Every need was met but this place lacked that relaxing, comforting feel of home.

The Drakos estate certainly wasn't where Popi had planned to end up after leaving the hospital, but with the island undergoing renovations and her parents stricken by the flu, Apollo's offer had seemed like the only logical offer.

They'd agreed to use the name their siblings had chosen for the baby, Sebastian. As it was quite a mouthful, they'd nicknamed the baby Seb. It suited him.

The mansion, on the other hand, took a lot to get used to it. The place was enormous. It was possible for them to both be home and not even run into each other. The home was older but it had been updated over the years with all the modern amenities without losing its classic charms.

Popi felt like she was living in a museum. Everything in this enormous foyer was some priceless work of art. This place was definitely more museum than home. No wonder her sister and brother-in-law had never considered living here, preferring a smaller house near the sea. And it in some way explained why Apollo never came home. This place, though stunning with its marble floors and soaring columns, was cold. It was the complete opposite of her own cozy, colorful and warm childhood home. And nothing like her bungalow on Infinity Island. In fact, her entire place could fit within the walls of the foyer alone.

Was the lack of hominess within the mansion the reason Apollo had made himself scarce since they'd brought the baby home a week ago? Or was he avoiding her? Did he regret extending an invitation to her while her parents were dealing with a string of illnesses?

Well, she was done being ignored. If Apollo wouldn't come to her, she would go to him. And that meant a trip to the gardens. It appeared to be his passion and, in all fairness, the gardens were more weeds than flowers or foliage. If someone didn't tend to them immediately, the weeds would win.

With the baby fed, changed and down for a nap, Popi left the nanny Apollo had insisted on hiring in charge and went to seek out her host. She made her way down the sweeping steps off the grand patio at the back of the home. She could see how this area had been stunning at one time, but time and the elements had done a number on just about everything.

Popi followed the stone path until she heard the sounds of work being done. To her surprise, Apollo wasn't out here alone. At least he'd had sense to call in a work crew, because an enormous garden like this would take him years to restore on his own.

After being pointed in the right direction, Popi came across Apollo adding dirt around the base of what she surmised to be a small fruit tree. And then as her gaze took in his shirtless appearance, her mouth grew dry. He looked good—too good.

His skin was deeply tanned. His corded muscles flexed as he moved a shovel of dirt from the wheelbarrow. No man had a right to look that good. She should just tiptoe backward and slip away. Because without his shirt on, she had a hard time stringing two thoughts together, much less trying to speak.

Apollo glanced up as though he sensed her presence. "Is something wrong? Is it the baby?"

"Uh…" *Come on, Popi. You can do better than that.* She swallowed hard. "The baby is fine." She forced a smile to her face as her insides shivered with nervous energy. "I promise."

It was sad that upon seeing her that he would jump to the conclusion that something was amiss. Was it such a leap for him to consider another reason for her being out here to see him?

She was right to have come here. If they were going to do this co-parenting thing, with the child splitting time between her on the island and Apollo here at the estate, they needed to be friends—not just two people who coexisted during a brutal storm. Even though he'd opened up to her that special night, he'd since shut down again. She hoped to bridge the gap once more.

Apollo's brows drew together. "Then why are you out here?"

Again, it was sad that he had to ask that question instead of just enjoying her company. She worried her bottom lip and glanced away. And then she wondered if coming here to the garden—to his private area—his sanctuary—had been a mistake.

"I came out here because… Well, I thought we, um…" Being near him was making her unusually nervous.

"How are you at gardening?" He turned back to the tree and finished packing the dirt.

"I, uh, don't have any experience. We always lived in the city, so the only plants we had were in pots in the windows. I must admit I never bothered with them. That was my mother's territory."

"It's never too late to learn." He gave her outfit a quick once-over. "But I'm sure you don't want to get your nice outfit all dirty."

She glanced down at her blue capris and white knit top. She did like this outfit. It fit her well and yet it was also comfortable. But she had a choice to make: stain her favorite outfit while making inroads with Apollo or walk away, leaving the awkward distance between them.

Without hesitation, Popi moved next to him and dropped down to her knees. "Where do we start?"

For the first time since Seb was born, Apollo smiled at her. "This sapling is done."

"Oh." A frown pulled at her lips. She must have misunderstood him.

"Don't worry. I have plenty more waiting to be planted." He got to his feet, pulled off his gloves and then held his hand out to her.

She placed her hand in his, and immediately a jolt of awareness raced up her arm and set her heart aflutter. Her gaze met his. The cool indifference that he'd shown her since they'd returned home with baby Seb was gone. In its place was warmth and, dare she say it, a twinkle of interest.

He led her to another secluded spot, where he'd already removed a patch of weeds and was ready to plant a lemon tree. Out here in the garden, he was chatty. So long as she supplied questions about anything pertaining to the garden, he gave her lengthy, informative answers.

Was it possible it was the house that put him in a sullen mood and not her? He did say he and his father had a turbulent past. Perhaps there were too many bad memories tied up in the house.

As they worked together, adding the water

around the roots, followed by the loose dirt, Popi asked, "Why did you return here?" When he sent her a puzzled look, she added, "You know—instead of selling the estate and getting a place, um…" She knew she had to be careful how she phrased this, as she didn't want to undo the progress they'd made so far. "Someplace smaller for just you…and Seb."

Relief filtered over his face as though he were expecting some other question. He shrugged and returned to adding the dirt back around the tree. "It's the Drakos estate. And I'm a Drakos. And this is Seb's home."

Where he had been giving her lengthy answers, she noticed that he'd reverted back to his short answers. She also noticed how he said this was the baby's home—not his. There was more he wasn't saying, but he didn't need to. He was drawn to this place because it was part of his heritage, but it was also mired in bad memories. She wondered if there was any way to untangle the two.

"Stop." Apollo's voice drew her from her musings.

"Stop what?" She glanced down at her hands, but she hadn't been doing anything.

"Not the gardening." He shook his head. "Stop trying to figure out ways to fix me. Some things and some people can't be fixed."

She didn't believe that. But she knew arguing with him would be pointless—

"Miss Costas?"

Popi glanced over her shoulder to find one of the young maids heading toward her. Popi got to her feet and brushed off the gloves that Apollo had loaned her. Apollo moved beside Popi with a concerned look on his face.

The young woman stopped in front of her. "You wanted to know when the baby woke up. He's up now and in a fine mood." The young girl looked at Apollo and blushed. "I should get back to the house."

Popi held back a laugh until the young woman was out of sight.

Apollo studied her. "What's so amusing?"

"Someone has a crush on you."

His gaze moved from her to the young maid and then back to Popi. He shook his head. "No."

"Yes. Didn't you see her blush?"

He noticeably swallowed. "I should probably replace her."

Popi shook her head. "Don't do that. I'm sure she needs the job. Besides, if you replace all of the females that have a crush on you, then you'd have a very small staff."

Apollo's mouth opened but nothing came out. He pressed his lips together. Was that a tinge of color in his cheeks?

"As long as you don't encourage her, you shouldn't have a problem with her."

CHAPTER SIXTEEN

THINGS WERE CHANGING...

For the better, she liked to think.

Popi refilled her coffee cup and moved to the terrace. Now that she knew about Apollo's passion for gardening and his willingness to teach her, she regularly joined him when Seb didn't need her.

But she found that their conversation centered on agriculture. And she simply didn't have the same passion for flowers and trees that Apollo did. She'd been hoping they would connect on a deeper level. Because if he couldn't connect with her, would he be able to do it with Seb?

She leaned back in the cushioned chair and sipped her morning coffee. The baby had already been up, eaten and played before going back down for a morning nap. That had been Popi's cue to grab some coffee before heading to the garden.

It was at Apollo's insistence a nanny had been hired. She was an older woman with years of experience and stellar references that were all veri-

Apollo's brow arched. "Who else should I be cautious around?"

Popi shrugged. She didn't want him to become even more withdrawn. This was the only maid to make her infatuation blatantly obvious.

"What about you?" he asked.

"What about me?" Suddenly she felt quite uncomfortable. Surely he wasn't asking what she thought.

His blue eyes studied her. "Do you have a secret crush on me too?"

"Uh…" The breath got caught in the back of her throat. And suddenly the sun was quite uncomfortably hot. "I should go check on the baby."

She turned and walked as fast as she could without breaking into a run. She should have answered him, but she hated lying. And there was no way she was admitting to him that she too had a crush on him, because it was nothing more than a rush of hormones.

After giving birth, her body was all over the place. Plus Apollo had helped her through the scariest, yet most profound moment of her life—giving birth to Seb. For that she would always be grateful to him.

Right now Apollo was just having some fun at her expense. Nothing more. His deep laughter followed her up the path. It wasn't like he was truly interested in her answer. Right?

fied. In the end, Popi realized that having another person devoted to the care and nurturing of Seb could only ever be a good thing. And it in no way detracted from her interactions with the baby.

"I thought I might find you here." Apollo's voice interrupted her thoughts.

She turned to find him approaching the empty chair next to hers. "I was beginning to wonder if you'd slept in."

"Not a chance. I've been getting up with the sun for so many years that I don't know if I could sleep late even if I needed to." He sat down. "I take it the baby had you up early."

She nodded. "I suppose he takes after his uncle."

A smile pulled at Apollo's lips. "Do you really think he's like me?"

"I think he looks a lot like you."

His smile broadened. "But I think you've totally won him over. Every time I pick him up, he cries. When you hold him, he's all smiles."

So, he'd noticed that too. She hadn't said anything about it, as she didn't want to make him feel bad. Seb was just as much Apollo's nephew as he was hers. They'd been dancing around the subject of a split-custody arrangement since they'd been discharged from the hospital.

She couldn't stay here forever. The repairs to Infinity Island were almost complete. They had to get the legal issues taken care of so that they could both move on. Because even though they'd become friends, there was nothing more to this arrangement than mutual respect for each other and their devotion to the baby.

"Apollo, we need to talk—"

"I agree. I've been giving this a lot of thought. And I think I've come to a solution."

"A solution?" Was he talking about the same thing as her?

He nodded. "We both love Seb. And he is the Drakos heir. That little boy will one day come into great wealth and wield unimaginable power."

She had an uneasy feeling in the pit of her stomach. When he started talking about the baby being the heir, she knew she was in trouble. Apollo was seeing Seb not as a sweet baby in need of love and nurturing but rather of the power that the baby will hold one day and the guardian that must handle the business affairs for the baby until its of age.

Apollo continued, even though she'd missed part of what he'd said. "It's for this reason that the baby should remain here—at the Drakos estate."

"I thought we'd agreed on split custody."

"I said I'd think about it. And I did. It'll will be less confusing for him to stay here at the estate. He'll have an entire staff to watch after him."

Popi set aside her coffee, no longer having the stomach for it. She sat up straight. "I didn't know that you still looked at Seb that way."

"What way? You mean as the heir?"

She nodded. "He's just a little baby." She waved her hand around. "None of this means anything to him."

Apollo's eyes became shuttered, blocking her out. "This place means everything. I may have walked away from here because I didn't feel as though I belonged here, but I never doubted the importance of the estate. My brother was always the chosen one. He was the one my father appointed to step into his shoes. And that role will now fall to my nephew."

That was a lot to put on a small, helpless baby. "But what about you?"

"I will help the army of trustees selected to run the business until Seb is old enough to take over."

"And then what? You're just going to turn your back on your family's business again?"

"Sure. Why not? It was not my calling like it was my brother's. Nile was the one obsessed with all things Drakos. He would want his son to be raised here."

"And what about you and your future children? Won't they want a place in the family business?"

He gave a firm shake of his head. "I'm not having children. I'm not going through that again."

"Through what?"

He glanced away. "Nothing."

"It was definitely something." She didn't understand why he would resolutely write off the possibility of children. He surely didn't think he would be climbing mountains and hiking the Amazon the rest of his life, did he? "Apollo, talk to me."

He looked at her with emotions reflected in his eyes. But she couldn't discern if it was anger at her for pushing the subject.

He cleared his throat. "I won't be responsible for another person dying."

"What?" Was he referring to his brother? If so, she didn't see how he could feel responsible. He wasn't even in the country at the time. Or was it someone else? "Who?"

A few seconds passed before he said, "My mother."

He killed his mother? No. That couldn't be right.

She was most definitely missing something.

Her gaze searched his face for answers but found none. "I don't understand."

He stared out at the vast landscaped yard with its elaborate water fountain and gorgeous flower garden. "My mother died after giving birth to me. And my father blamed me for her death until his own dying breath."

Suddenly she understood him so much better. This was why he was always on a new adventure. Who would want to stick around to be blamed for something that was in no way his fault?

Popi reached out, placing her hand on his arm. "Surely you understand that it wasn't your fault."

"I understand that I was an accident. Once my father got my brother, he wasn't interested in having more children, but he was willing to indulge my mother. But when it all went so horribly wrong, I was blamed. I was just a child but I knew my father hated me."

"He didn't hate you." She just couldn't believe that was true. Could a parent really hate their child? She couldn't accept such a horrible reality for him. "Your father was grieving his wife."

Apollo turned a haunted look at her. "For years?" He shook his head. "I don't think so."

"I'm sorry you lived through that."

"I had my brother. He did his best to shield me. He stood up to my father when I wasn't old enough to do it myself."

"I had no idea you and your brother were that close."

"We used to be. In fact, we used to play hide-and-seek out in the gardens. I was good at hiding. My brother, not so much. We used to have all sorts of adventures out there."

"And this place, it reminds you of those times?" She couldn't help but ask. She'd noticed he spent a great amount of time either running errands or working in the gardens. If he kept working outside, she was pretty certain the entire grounds, and that was a massive amount of property, would end up being one enormous exotic garden.

He rubbed the back of his neck. "I guess. My brother inherited the controlling shares of the family business, while I inherited a much smaller share and this estate."

"I understand now why you think Seb should be raised here, but what about my sister's wishes?" Andrina wasn't here to speak for her herself and without a will, Popi had to do it. Because they might not have been blood relatives, but they were as close as two sisters could be. "She would want her son to know me…to have a mother figure… someone who understands that families come in all shapes and sizes. His family will be different than most of his friends', but his life will be filled with love that he can always count on."

Apollo nodded in agreement. "You are right. So, you think it is best for him to split time between here and Infinity Island?"

She smiled, knowing she'd finally gotten through to him. And then she nodded.

"Or you could stay here."

"Here?" The smile slipped from her face. Was he serious? "With you?"

"That's the general idea, but I can see you don't like the idea."

"It's just that my career…my home…it's back on the island." She loved Seb, but she loved her job too. She didn't want to have to pick one over the other. And living here with Apollo, knowing the chemistry between them—it was a recipe for disaster.

"Keep my offer in mind. This mansion is more than big enough for both of us." He paused as though waiting for her to respond, but she didn't know what to say. She'd been caught off guard. And so he continued. "Speaking of the mansion, I keep forgetting to tell you that I've started a household account in your name."

"My name?"

He nodded. "It's so you can set up the nursery any way you want. Feel free to paint, buy new drapes or whatever you want. If there isn't enough, let me know."

He was now Seb's financial guardian. Plus from what she'd gleaned about him on the internet, Apollo came with his own great wealth. Still, it felt weird to take money from him. She was used to standing on her own feet and paying her own way. She'd been doing that ever since she finished college. And she liked her independence.

But then she realized the money, though under her control, wasn't for her. It was for the baby. And the nursery really could use an overhaul. The white paint was now yellowing. There were some cracks. And the windows stuck when she tried to open them to let in some fresh air. They definitely needed to be replaced.

"Thank you. The nursery could use some sprucing up. I'll try not to spend much."

Apollo smiled at her, making her stomach flip. "You don't have to worry about the money. Do what needs to be done. I'll cover it."

She was used to living on a budget. Things in Apollo's world—and now Seb's—were a lot different. "I better get started with the plans. I want to make sure I have time to finish the room."

Soon she'd be returning to Infinity Island. She hoped they were able to repair all of the damage from the storm and make it as though it had never happened.

The truth was that she wasn't homesick for the island like she'd thought she'd be. In truth, she liked it here at Apollo's home. And it had nothing to do with living in a mansion that was straight out of the movies. Or the fact that Apollo had insisted on employing a household staff the size of a small army—

"I must be going." He abruptly got to his feet. The smile had faded from his face. "I have a new shipment of plants arriving today."

"Are you creating your own exotic jungle?" She meant it to tease him, but it did nothing to soften the frown now pulling at his lips.

"Perhaps." And with that he walked away.

She could tell it was killing him to stay here. And that saddened her. When they'd been on Infinity Island, he'd been happier, but now it was like a dark cloud was following him. It wasn't good for him and it certainly wasn't good for Seb to see Apollo so unhappy.

And if Apollo was unhappy living at the estate, it meant when the baby was with her, Apollo would be off on another dangerous adventure. She told herself she was upset on behalf of the baby that would miss him, but she wasn't that good of a liar. She would miss him too. And she worried that his body wasn't healed enough and he would reinjure himself.

While she pondered how or even if it was possible to fix this problem, she drank the last of her coffee and got to her feet. She had a room to make over. It was a task she welcomed. It would keep her from thinking about the sexy man with the eye-catching tattoo that wrapped around his sculpted bicep, and his deep, sexy voice that made her insides melt.

What had he been thinking?

Two weeks later, the nursery was nearly finished. Popi was astonished at the amount of money Apollo had set aside to redo the room. Even with a rush order for new windows, doors, fixtures and paint, it had barely made a dent in the amount. She'd been about to return the remainder of the funds, but then she had a thought.

What if she was to give the rest of the home a makeover?

At first she'd dismissed the idea. As this wasn't her home, it wasn't up to her to redecorate. But something told her Apollo never would. It wasn't his thing. He spent almost every waking hour outdoors.

But she could see how uncomfortable he was when he was inside. He'd frown at a portrait and then turn away. He'd avoid the study altogether. There were many rooms which he didn't visit or would only step into for just a moment or two.

As the idea took root, she just couldn't dismiss it. If she could help Apollo get past his bad memories and not have them constantly pop up in his mind, she felt compelled to do it. What else could she do until Infinity Island was back up and running? She wasn't used to having idle time.

Organizing and creating visions was her job. Sure, she normally did it in the form of a wedding, but she was certain she could take those skills and create a home that didn't make Apollo feel like running back to the Amazon as soon as he walked in the door. Or keep him outside digging up more and more of the grounds to create the biggest and most impressive garden in the region. People were starting to say that the gardens were going to rival the mansion in size and elaborateness. And Popi had to agree. The gardens were breathtaking.

So, that evening at dinner, Popi brought up the subject of repainting and updating some of the other rooms with the extra money. Apollo gave her the go-ahead with his blessing.

And so she started in a wing that Apollo didn't visit. One room led to another room, putting portraits and decorative pieces in storage and replacing them with pieces more in line with Apollo's tastes, from animal prints to foliage paintings. The paint on the wall was warmer, and accent walls with vibrant colors were done.

A few weeks later, she'd completed a cosmetic makeover of the east wing of the mansion, but she wasn't ready to show Apollo what she'd accomplished—not yet. She wanted to work on the study first.

When the house phone rung, Popi rushed for it. But when she picked it up, Apollo spoke before she could. Popi remained quiet. She was expecting a call from the home-interiors store about some specialty wallpaper that she'd chosen to create a very special accent wall in Apollo's study. She waited to see if this was in fact the store calling.

"Apollo, is that you?"

There was a slight pause.

"Matias?"

"It's me, buddy. I hadn't heard from you in a while—"

Popi was disappointed that the call wasn't about the order, as they couldn't progress with the study until she was certain the store could get enough of a particular wallpaper. Hopefully they would call soon. If she could get Apollo to relax in his home, maybe he wouldn't be so eager to head out on his next adventure.

Popi moved to hang up the phone when something caught her attention. The man, Matias, said, "…you joining me on my next safari. And I'm just about to head out."

"A safari. I've always wanted to do that but never had the chance."

"Well, this is your chance."

"So it is."

That's all Popi needed to hear. Her hand moved quickly to slam down the phone in frustration, but she stopped herself just before placing the phone on the receiver. Instead she hung up gently, all the while mulling over what she'd learned.

So nothing they'd shared meant anything to him. He was just putting in time until what? The baby was comfortable with the household staff? Or was he going to ask her to watch Seb every time he got the urge for an adventure?

The blood warmed in her veins. Sure, she'd love having the extra time with Seb, but the baby wasn't a possession to be passed around at will. Eventually Seb would start asking questions. She was about to go momma bear on Apollo. He needed to be a devoted parent to Seb, not just a guardian of the child's vast inheritance. If that was too much for Apollo to handle, then she would raise Seb on her own.

And then there was the thing between them. The way he looked at her when he didn't think she was paying attention and the way he flirted with her, it had to mean something, right? Or was she building up this relationship in her mind when in fact it was nothing to him? Something to pass the time? Or was it something more sinister? Was he trying to win her over so that she wouldn't fight him for the baby?

She immediately dismissed the idea. Apollo may not see a future for them, but he wasn't devious. He was kind. And he was thoughtful. She'd never believe that he had an ulterior motive.

Did that make her foolish? She hoped not. But she needed to stop concentrating so much on making this stone-cold mansion into a warm, inviting home and worry more about getting back to Infinity Island.

She rushed downstairs to confront him, but as she searched room after room, she realized that she'd missed him. Seb shouldn't be left with a nanny. He needed to live with her on Infinity Island, where there was an entire village of extended family and friends. She dialed the number of her attorney—the one who had handled things after her sister and brother-in-law's deaths.

Popi probably should have waited to phone until she'd calmed down. Maybe then she wouldn't have had to pay the attorney's steep fees to listen to her vent about Apollo, their messy situation and her concerns about him leaving the country.

She didn't want Apollo to leave. She thought that they were growing closer. But had she only seen what she wanted? Was Apollo the same carefree, free spirit he'd always been?

CHAPTER SEVENTEEN

HE NEEDED OUT of the house.

The only problem was, he hadn't wanted to walk out the door.

Apollo's car sped down the road. He never thought he would want to stay at the mansion. But it wasn't the same place as when he was growing up. It was different now—now that Popi and Seb were there. The sound of laughter was now common around the house. And each morning all the drapes were pulled back, flooding the mansion with bright, rejuvenating sunshine.

At first he'd started working on the neglected gardens as a way of getting out of the house, but now he had to force himself to go work on the project. He'd much rather stay inside and follow Popi around. But he knew that was a fool's errand.

Popi was planning to leave the estate—leave him—just as soon as Infinity Island's updates were completed. The closer the time for her departure came, the more he realized he didn't want her to leave.

He'd even considered giving her a reason to stay—with him. The only reason he'd resisted the urge was knowing he couldn't give her what she wanted. Long-term relationships didn't work out for him. Every one that he'd had ended in disaster. And he wouldn't subject Seb to a broken home.

Apollo slowed the car as he neared the *bistrot* where he was to meet up with Matias. He found a parking spot on the busy street and slipped his black Greek supercar into the spot.

As he walked into the darkened *bistrot*, he realized he should have turned Matias down on the phone. His life had changed and his wings had been clipped.

An image of Seb filled his mind. He knew that giving up his old nomadic ways was for the best. He loved Seb with all his heart. But sometimes he let himself imagine what his next adventure might entail—until his thoughts turned to holding Seb in his arms. Then Apollo knew he was right where he belonged—embarking on the most important adventure of his life.

Matias waved from across the room.

Apollo made his way to him, ordering a dark ale on his way. He took a seat across the table from a friend he'd made while trekking through Nepal. He'd met so many interesting people along his travels. In an effort to keep people from flocking to him because of his family's fortune, he typically used his mother's maiden name. Some would exchange information, along with a promise to keep in contact, but it was rare he would hear from anyone again. Matias was different.

They had kept in contact over the past eight years. Like him, Matias's family was influential in Madrid. It made it easy for them to open up to each other because neither wanted anything from the other. And along the way, they found they had a lot in common, like avoiding commitments, not living up to family expectations and enjoying the thrill of an adventure.

"Hey, man." Matias got to his feet. They clutched hands, pulled each other close and, with their free hands, clapped each other on the back. They quickly pulled apart. "It's good to see you, man. I mean it's really good to see you."

"Thanks. I'm surprised to see you in Athens."

"I'm just passing through. After I heard about your accident, I wanted to see that you're truly in one piece."

They both sat down and a waitress brought their drinks. Apollo took a sip of the dark brew. "Yeah. That was a bad one. Doctors weren't sure if I was going to make it or not."

"I would have been there for you if I had known about it."

Apollo shook off the idea. "There was nothing you could do. Nothing anyone could do. It just took time."

"And so you've decided to spend some time at home?"

With reluctance, he told Matias about his brother's death and the new baby. He skimmed over the subject of Popi. He wasn't sure how to describe his relationship with her. Was that right? Did they have a relationship?

His mind slipped back to the steamy kisses they'd shared. And they'd have shared so much more if not for her pregnancy. But did that equate to a relationship?

Then again, they were sharing a home. And they were sharing a baby, not to mention the time they spent gardening together and the meals they shared. The more these facts piled up, the harder it got for him to stick his head in the sand and refuse to accept what was right in front of him.

He was involved in a romantic relationship with Popi. And he was committed to being a full-time father to Seb.

His heart stilled for a moment as the significance of this acknowledgment settled in his mind. But where did it go from here? Where did he want it to go? Would Popi stay at the estate with him if he asked her?

"Hey." Matias waved his hand in front of Apollo, gaining his attention. "Where'd you go?"

"What?" He had no idea what Matias had been

saying. That wasn't like him. But this was a situation that he'd never been in before. "Sorry. I guess I just have a lot on my mind."

"It sounds like it. So, what's her name?"

Apollo frowned. "Why do you just assume it's a woman?"

"Because I know you. And there's a look on your face—"

"What look?"

Matias smiled and shook his head. "Never mind."

"I do mind. What look?"

"Like you're a lovesick pup—"

"I'm not!" The denial came so quick and so vehemently that even he didn't believe it.

Matias's eyes widened as he held up his hands. "Hey, you asked." He glanced down at the table. "So, back to the reason for my visit. How soon are you ready to set off on a new excursion? I've got guides set up for a walking safari. We'll get up close and personal with the wildlife."

It was something that Apollo had never done. And it was something that he'd always wanted to do. But he'd never found it challenging enough. Until now, he'd always wanted to push himself to the edge. But with this last adventure, he'd gotten too close to the edge and it had cost him.

The safari was exactly what he needed while his body continued to heal. But that would mean leaving Seb. That was something he couldn't do.

It was up to him to look after the little guy. And more than that—he'd miss Seb something awful.

He shook his head. "I can't, man."

"You mean because of your injuries?"

"No. I mean I'm still not one hundred percent, but I have the baby now. I have to put him first. I owe that much to my brother."

But that wasn't exactly the truth. His desire to stay here in Athens wasn't born out of duty but rather out of desire. He wanted to stay home—to be there with Seb—and Popi. To share his life with them.

Matias stared at him. "Is that the only reason holding you here?"

"What else would there be?" Popi's beautiful face filled his mind, but he quickly dismissed it.

"I don't know, but you have that look on your face again."

Finally deciding that he needed some advice about his situation with Popi, he opened up to his friend. He told Matias about the first time he met Popi and that undeniable immediate attraction. He went on to mention that Popi's life was on Infinity Island and how she planned to return to her life there as soon as possible—with the baby. And how he would once again be alone.

"You'd be able to get back to your adventures," Matias offered.

Apollo lowered his gaze and stared blindly into his drink. "I don't know if it was almost dying on this last excursion or what, but I'm not anxious to get back out there. At least not yet."

"Is it that? Or have you finally found a reason to stay at home?"

"You mean Popi?" When Matias nodded, Apollo said, "But this arrangement is about to end and then she'll be gone." Just like everyone else in his life.

"Unless you give her a reason to stay."

Apollo looked up at his friend, finding that he was perfectly serious. But what could he offer Popi to stay here? Her career and friends were on the island. When she spoke of the island and the weddings she'd planned, it was obvious how much she missed it.

But her family was here in Athens. A flicker of hope sparked within him. If he were able to give her another reason, maybe he could change her mind. But how?

He searched his mind to come up with some reason that would rival her desire to return to Infinity Island. There had to be an answer. It wasn't like money would be an obstacle. But he also knew throwing money at Popi wouldn't be the answer. She was so stubbornly independent.

"Can I offer you a bit of advice?" When Apollo nodded, Matias said, "Be careful. I know things seem really good now. But move cautiously. I just got burned by a woman who was only interested in my bank account. She put on such a good show that I didn't see it. I was just about to propose to her when I learned the truth."

"Is this the reason you missed the last trip?"

It was Matias's turn to avoid Apollo's gaze as he nodded.

"It's just as well. As you can tell, it didn't go well." Apollo rubbed his surgically repaired thigh, which still had a dull ache to it.

"Just be careful is all I'm saying. Make sure if you move forward with her that she's interested in you and not what you can offer her."

Apollo didn't believe it was the case with Popi. He was certain she had a heart of gold. He pushed his friend's advice to the back of his mind.

"This place is more impressive than I ever could have imagined."

Two days later, Popi's mother stood in the nursery, holding Seb while gazing out the window at the estate grounds. The nursery had an excellent view of the extravagant gardens that Apollo was creating. Popi joined her mother at the window. She gazed down, catching a glimpse of Apollo as he worked in the bright sunshine without a shirt on.

He was too far away to make out the detailed lines of his well-defined muscles. But the memory of him working shirtless was vividly imprinted upon her mind. She'd been tempted more than once to reach out and smooth the flecks of dirt from his tanned skin, but each time she'd resisted the urge, unsure of his reaction.

Sure, they'd kissed, but she still didn't understand where that left them—except for wanting more. And since she'd had the baby, he'd been so reserved around her—even if she saw the desire reflected in his eyes. It wasn't like he was going to stay here in Athens. He was a nomad, always on to the next adventure.

"Looks like you find it impressive too." Her mother's voice drew Popi out of her thoughts.

"Mmm… What?"

Her mother sent her a knowing smile.

"What?" Popi asked.

"I'm thinking you're enjoying the view a little too much."

Heat rushed to Popi's chest and headed north to her cheeks. "I… I don't know what you mean."

Her mother arched a brow. "Popi, don't play coy with me. I saw you looking at Apollo. Is there more to this playing house than caring for Seb?"

"Of course not." Did her response sound like a lie? Because it sure felt like one.

Disbelief reflected in her mother's eyes. "Just make sure that whatever you do with Apollo, it's for the right reason."

That was it? No lecture? No telling her that he was absolutely the wrong person for her? Popi struggled to keep her mouth from gaping open.

"What?" Her mother placed the sleeping baby in the crib before turning back to her daughter.

"It's just that I expected you to tell me not to get involved with him…to stay away from a man who never slept in the same place more than a few nights."

"Is that what you expected me to say? Or is that what you've been saying to yourself?"

Popi shrugged, not wanting to answer. "I don't know what to make of him. He's so much different than the picture Andrina painted of him."

"That happens a lot. People are never quite what other people say of them. Usually there's so much more if you look beneath the surface."

Popi moved to a basket of fresh baby clothes and began placing them in the new chest of drawers. "It was so much easier when I was certain he was an irresponsible playboy, out to have a good time instead of taking responsibility for himself and his family. But now…"

"Now you've found out there might be reasons for his globetrotting."

Popi stopped and turned to her mother. "How did you know?"

"Your sister. She didn't know the whole story, but from what she was able to glean, Apollo had a harsh childhood, with an alcoholic father."

"She knew there was more to him?"

Her mother sighed. "She didn't know for sure, but she hoped when the time came that he would step up and be there for the family. And perhaps have a family of his own."

This was all so unexpected. Her sister had never said anything like this to her. In fact, Andrina had warned her, should she ever meet Apollo, to be on her guard. Maybe Popi had misinterpreted that warning. Maybe her sister had known just how dashing her brother-in-law was and she worried that Popi would fall for him and he would end up breaking her heart. Was that going to happen?

Had she already lost her heart to him? Was that why she was still here even though she'd received word that all the renovations had been completed on her bungalow?

She looked at her mother, who was wise in the ways of the heart. "But how am I to know what he wants?"

"The question you have to answer first is what do you want?"

"I… I don't know."

"Listen to your heart—it will guide you."

"If only it was that easy." But every time she listened to her heart, her mind intervened with all of the reasons that pursuing anything with Apollo wouldn't work.

"Don't push yourself. You've been through a lot, and so has he. But I have to say that your sister would be so proud of you."

Popi's heart stuttered. How could she be so caught up with Apollo? It wasn't right.

If it wasn't for her sister's death, she wouldn't be here. And Andrina wouldn't have died if it hadn't been for her. Which meant that she didn't deserve Apollo. She didn't deserve to have the perfect family that her sister had been robbed of.

"No, she wouldn't." Popi couldn't meet her mother's gaze. "Andrina should be here, not me."

"That's nonsense. I know that it's hard without your sister. I miss her every day. But one life is not more important than the other. I love you both, equally."

Her mother's unconditional love is what had gotten her through so much in life, including her sister's death. But there was something her mother didn't know—that she was the one who'd insisted that her sister be on that boat. She just didn't know how to admit to something so horrible.

"Mum, there's something you don't know—"

Knock-knock.

Apollo stuck his head in the doorway. "I heard we had company."

Introductions were made, and as though the baby sensed Apollo was in the room, Seb fussed, wanting to be picked up. Apollo readily lifted the baby into his arms as though Seb had always belonged there.

She noticed how Apollo had changed into

clean clothes. Still, he had the worst timing. But then again, maybe it was for the best. Her mother would just end up trying to make Popi feel better for what had happened to her sister. Her mother wouldn't throw around blame—that wasn't her way. And Popi didn't deserve her mother's sympathy and understanding.

And most of all, she didn't deserve Apollo… no matter how much she wished it was otherwise. Because this was the life her sister should have been living—an adoring man, a beautiful home and a smiling, happy baby.

Popi thought she was coming to terms with losing her sister and learning to live with the loss, but every time she held Seb and that little boy stared up at her with those big brown eyes—so much like Andrina's—the guilt washed over her.

She was the reason Andrina was on that boat. Popi's ultimatum was the only reason her sister had reluctantly gone out on the water. And that was why Popi couldn't let herself enjoy a family that was hers out of default. It wasn't right. Andrina should be here, watching her beautiful baby boy grow.

CHAPTER EIGHTEEN

HE COULDN'T SLEEP.

It wasn't from worry. And it wasn't from unpleasant memories.

In fact, it was quite the opposite.

For the first time in his life, Apollo was content and happy right here at home. He never thought that could happen. In fact, he had been quite certain that returning to the Drakos estate would be like a life sentence of misery.

And all this happiness was due to Popi.

His friend's warning about Popi echoed in his mind. He quickly dismissed it. Matias didn't know Popi. If he did, he'd realize she would never intentionally hurt anyone. After all, she even rescued helpless kittens.

She was like a ray of sunshine on a cloudy day. She could make something as mundane as breakfast be like a grand meal with her comical stories of Seb, her radiant smiles and her genuine interest in him. No one before her had ever taken such an interest in his life—not even his brother.

And he didn't want to miss a moment of the sunshine Popi had brought to his life.

Because he knew in the end that this wasn't going to last. This peaceful serenity that had taken over his life would end as soon as Popi walked out the door. And then what? He'd long to escape once again on one of his adventures?

But there was Seb to think of. He couldn't just leave him—not even with the best nanny or Anna, the housekeeper. No, Seb was his responsibility—his and Popi's. Because what he was quickly learning was that the baby needed both of them.

And then a thought began to percolate in his sleep-deprived mind. But it was so far out there that he was certain it was all fantasy without any substance. Because there was no way Popi would want a future with him. Would she?

"Waah... Waah... Waah... Waah..."

There was no time to answer the question. He obviously wasn't the only one not sleeping. Apollo sprang out of bed and headed for the nursery that was situated between his and Popi's bedrooms. He hoped to get there before Seb woke Popi too. There was no point in them both being awake.

Not taking the time to dress, Apollo rushed out of the bedroom in nothing more than his blue-and-white boxers. After all, the whole mansion was asleep. No one would see him. And Seb needed him.

Apollo rushed into the nursery. He immediately turned off the baby monitor so as not to wake Popi. She needed her rest. He'd noticed her at dinner and she had been quieter than normal. She'd even yawned through the main course. Maybe he'd been spending too much time in the garden and leaving her to deal with the baby more than he should. He made a mental note to be on hand more instead of losing track of time in the gardens.

"Hey, little man. It's okay." Apollo spoke softly as he picked up the baby. He cradled Seb against his bare shoulder. "What's the matter?"

Seb's crying softened but it didn't stop.

"Did you have a bad dream?" As he lightly bounced the baby in an effort to comfort him, he noticed that Seb's diaper was wet. A problem that he could solve. The nurse had instructed him on how to do this in the hospital. Between Popi and the nanny, he didn't have time to put the lesson to use until now.

"I see the problem. You need a diaper change. No problem. We've got this."

Until this point, he never thought he'd want a baby—another human counting on him for everything was daunting. But Seb was teaching him that he was capable of being there for someone— did that include Popi?

The baby's cry had woken her.

Popi hadn't moved at first. One book she'd read

about parenting said not to rush to the baby at their first cry. Sometimes the baby would self-soothe and go back to sleep. Waiting didn't come natural to her. Her natural tendency was to rush to the nursery and comfort Seb. But she wanted to be a good parent—the best possible—even if it wasn't always easy.

But the sound of Apollo's voice over the monitor surprised her. Usually that man slept like a log and didn't hear a thing. It didn't bother her. She'd opted to take the baby monitor so she could keep a close eye on Seb. She didn't want a nanny soothing the baby at night. Seb needed his mom holding him and letting him know that all would be right in the world again.

Popi sat up in bed, waiting to see if her assistance was needed, but then the baby monitor went totally silent. Apollo must have turned it off.

She knew he deserved some one-on-one time with the baby. It was good for both him and Seb. Since they'd returned from the hospital, Seb had grown a strong bond with Apollo. In the beginning, Seb would cry when Apollo picked him up, but now the baby would fuss for Apollo to hold him. At least that's the way it seemed to her. But she couldn't help worrying that Apollo would need help.

She'd never worried this much in her life. She was constantly thinking of ways to keep Seb safe or happy. She wondered if this was how it felt to truly be a mother. At times it could be exhausting. But the when Seb smiled, he made all of it worthwhile. He was a bundle of love.

Popi couldn't go back to sleep. She had to know what was going on, so she slipped out of bed and put on her robe. She tiptoed into the hallway, not wanting to startle Apollo or the baby. She paused at the doorway to the nursery. Apollo was inside with his bare back to her, as he had Seb on the changing table.

"I've got this, little guy. We'll have you all dried up in no time."

Popi enjoyed watching her two guys together. She quickly realized her mistake. Apollo wasn't her guy, even if they were living together and had shared a life-changing moment on the island—not to mention the toe-curling kiss beneath the stars.

With the soiled diaper off and the baby cleaned up, Apollo said, "Hang on, I just have to get a fresh diaper."

With one hand on the baby, he bent over to grab a fresh diaper off the lower shelf. Popi was about to say something when Apollo straightened and the baby peed—all over Apollo.

Popi couldn't help it—she burst out laughing.

Apollo turned a frown in her direction. "You saw that, huh?"

"Uh-huh." She stepped farther into the room and wiped the tears of laughter from her eyes. "I should have warned you to always have a fresh diaper ready so that doesn't happen. I can finish so you can go clean up."

He shook his head. "I'll finish changing him."

Apollo dried off, cleaned up the little guy again and then put a fresh diaper on him before handing Seb off to her. Holding the baby in her arms felt so right—so natural. So did sharing this moment with Apollo. They seemed like—dare she think it—a real family.

And the sight of Apollo standing there in nothing more than his briefs—*wow*, it had grown warm in the room. She resisted the urge to fan herself as she took in the view of his muscular chest and his six-pack abs. There were a few scars on him that she longed to run her fingers over and ask him about their origin, but she resisted the urge. Those scars only added to his sexy factor. They definitely didn't detract.

"We've got a lot to learn, little man." Apollo's voice drew her from her thoughts. "But we'll work on it."

When Apollo stepped forward to kiss the baby on the head, his lips came so close to hers. Was it her imagination or did he pause ever so slightly as though considering kissing her too?

Their gazes connected. The breath caught in her throat. She willed him to kiss her again.

If not for the baby in the crook of her arm, she would have looped her hands around Apollo's neck and pulled him down to her level. And then she would—

Apollo's head turned away. He kissed the baby good-night and headed for the shower. Popi was left standing there with her heart racing madly and the realization that she wanted this relationship to be more than two people sharing a space. She wanted the one thing she didn't deserve— this family.

CHAPTER NINETEEN

SHE WAS SOMETHING SPECIAL.

Very special.

And it wasn't just some pumped-up compliment to cover for all Popi had done by not only giving birth to his nephew but also her willingness to come here and make a home for the baby. Apollo really meant it. Popi was special. With every day that passed, he realized just how much Popi was changing his life, in big and little ways.

Most of all, he found that staying here in Athens was nothing like he'd originally envisioned. He found himself anxious to get up in the morning to seek out Popi and to hold Seb. He found that gardening was something he really enjoyed. He'd learned a lot about vegetation while he was off on his adventures from both the tour guides and the locals. And now he was able to put that knowledge to use.

He had a very special evening in mind for Popi. It was his way of thanking her for giving him a new outlook on life. And he'd worked on this plan all day, including a trip to the barber. His longish hair was now cut short. Everything had to be perfect for her.

As afternoon faded to evening, he rushed through the shower, shaved not once but twice and dressed in some dark jeans and a white collared shirt with the sleeves rolled up. He stopped in front of the mirror, which was something he seldom did, but tonight was different. Tonight he had to look decent—no, he had to look good. Really good. Popi deserved nothing less. He swept his fingers through his hair and then he was out the door.

He located Popi in the nursery. She placed the baby in the crib for a nap. Seb had a set routine. A nap before his evening feeding and then he'd stay awake for the late show and go down for the night, not waking up again until morning.

"I was looking for you," Apollo said.

Popi put a finger to her lips. "Shh…"

Apollo mouthed *sorry*.

She nodded in understanding, but didn't speak until they'd quietly backed out of the room. With great care, she eased the nursery door closed.

She turned to him. "What did you need?"

"You." He'd already made sure the nanny would keep an eye on Seb for the rest of the evening.

"Me." Her beautiful eyes widened. "For what?"

"It's a surprise."

"I... I don't know if I'm up for it."

"Sure you are. Come on. I promise you'll like it." At least he hoped she would.

He didn't give her time to talk herself out of joining him. He took her hand in his, liking the way her skin felt next to his. He laced his fingers with hers as though it was something they'd been doing for years. And then he started for the grand staircase.

At the top of the stairs, Popi stopped. "Wait. I don't even know where we're going. Is it dressy?"

"Not unless you want it to be."

It was then that she noticeably took in his attire. Her gaze skimmed down over one of his dressier shirts and down to his newest pair of jeans. When her gaze finally met his, there was a hint of pink in her cheeks. The color only enhanced her beauty.

"See anything you like?" He couldn't help himself from teasing her.

"You...you've changed. Your hair is all cut off. You even shaved. And you're dressed up. You look incredibly handsome. Did you do all of this for me?" When he nodded, her cheeks turned a deeper hue of pink. "Then I have to change. I can't go anywhere like this. I have baby drool on my shirt."

"I promise no one will notice."

She frowned at him. "I'll notice."

She pulled her hand from his, turned and then headed back down the hallway.

Apollo sighed. He didn't have the patience to wait around for her. Actually it was more than that. He was afraid the baby would wake up and then Popi would refuse to leave Seb until he was asleep again.

But Apollo knew his anxiety ran deeper than that. He was afraid he would come up with an excuse not to follow through with his plan. It felt like he was standing at the edge of a two-hundred-foot cliff and getting ready to step off with nothing but water to catch him.

Even though his gut was twisted up with nervous tension, he couldn't walk away. He had to see if this thing growing between them was real or not. Because today marked six weeks since Seb's birth, and Popi had just been to the doctor's and gotten the all clear. Apollo no longer had to hold her at arm's length or worry about things getting out of control between them. Tonight was a new beginning for them.

While Popi changed clothes, Apollo rushed to the kitchen just to check on things. Nothing could go wrong with this evening. He owed Popi a memorable night.

To his relief, the food was all on track. Now he just hoped Popi didn't change her mind. However, when he returned to the foyer, he found Popi standing there in a sleeveless black-and-white high-low dress. With her hair pinned up, she looked like a runway model. She took his breath away.

"I hope this is all right," she said. "I picked it up when I was in the city."

"It's better than all right. You look stunning."

His compliment brought a smile to her kissable lips, and his heart thumped against his ribs. It was all he could do to hold himself back and not take her in his arms right then and there. But he assured himself there would be plenty of time for that later.

He stepped up to her and pulled a black silk handkerchief from his pocket. "Turn around."

The smile fell from her face. A worried look reflected in her eyes. "What's that for?"

"It wouldn't be a surprise if you saw it." When his words did nothing to ease the stress lines etching around her eyes, he said, "Trust me. You will like this."

Her gaze moved from the blindfold to him. "Couldn't I just close my eyes?"

He smiled and shook his head. "You'll peek."

"No, I won't."

"Liar." He sent her a teasing smile.

Her mouth gaped in mock outrage.

"Don't give me that look," he said. "We've been living together for a while and I know that you're terrible with surprises."

"I am not."

"Really?" He arched a challenging brow. "Then how come you told me that I couldn't see the nursery before you'd finished with it, but then you showed me the paint and then the crib and then—"

"Okay. Okay. So I get excited sometimes and it's hard to keep it to myself."

"Uh-huh. Hence the blindfold." He gestured for her to turn around.

She hesitated.

"You don't want to miss the surprise, do you?"

Without a word, she turned around and let him affix the blindfold. He was careful not to draw the loose curls of her hair into the knot. And then he tucked her hand securely in the crook of his arm. Joined together, he led her outside to the garden.

"Where are we going?" Popi asked.

"You'll see soon."

They continued walking. He was careful to keep her from walking into the statues in the garden or from running into any garden walls or vegetation.

"This isn't the way to the car."

"No, it's not."

"So we're walking to the destination?" When he didn't respond, she said, "Apollo, at least give me a hint."

He stopped walking. He glanced around, making sure that everything was how he'd envisioned. To his great relief, it was.

"Apollo? What is it? Would you say something?" She tugged on his arm.

A smile lifted his lips. "Is someone impatient?"

"Yes."

She sniffed the air. "Mmm… It smells so sweet."

He'd made sure to include some aromatic flowers in every part of the garden. He'd wanted it to be a more-than-visual experience.

"Okay. Stand still." He moved behind her and removed the blindfold.

Popi gasped.

She stepped forward, checking out the table for two in the garden path. The table was set with white linen and candles. She glanced back at him. "You did all of this for me?"

He nodded. "Do you like it?"

"I love it." Her gaze lifted to the glass lanterns with candles dangling from tree branches.

Those had been a bit more of a challenge than he'd been planning, as he'd had to move the dinner spot to an older section of the garden, where the trees were mature enough to handle the weight of the lanterns. In the background, a romantic ballad was carried by the gentle breeze.

"This is much more than a little something."

He held his hand out to her. "Would you care to dance?"

Without a word, she slipped her hand in his and he drew her close. His arm wrapped around her slender waist, while his other hand wrapped around hers. Their bodies swayed together as the sun sank below the horizon and the lanterns cast streaks of light across the garden.

She lifted her head so that her gaze met his. It was then that he realized how close they were. If he were to lean just a little bit forward, he could kiss her. The temptation lured him. But he wondered how Popi would react. Would she welcome the advance? Or would she push him away?

The look in her eyes wasn't telling him anything. Had he always been this bad at reading women? Or was it his worry about messing things up with Popi that had him second-guessing his every move with her?

"Why did you do this?" she asked. "It's so special—so amazing."

"Because I wanted to make you smile." And it did make her smile.

Before he could say more and explain how much she'd come to mean to him, their dinner arrived. A parade of three servers carried covered trays and placed them on the small table.

Apollo held his arm out to her. "Shall we?"

Popi once more placed her hand in the crook of his arm and let him escort her to the table, where he pulled out her chair. As they enjoyed the meal, the lanterns cast a warm glow around them. It was as if they were in their own secret world.

He glanced down to find her moving the food around her plate. "Don't you like the food?"

Her gaze lifted. "It's delicious."

"Then why are you barely eating?"

"I'm sorry." She took a bite.

The magic of the evening was slipping away and he desperately wanted to get it back. There was something weighing on Popi's mind, but how did he get her to open up to him? Was it something he'd done? Was this cozy dinner a bad idea?

This was the sweetest gesture anyone had ever done for her.

And she didn't deserve it.

If only he knew the truth.

Popi couldn't get the conversation with her mother out of her mind. Everyone seemed to think she was someone great, but the truth was she was not—not even close. She felt like a total imposter.

"I think they're playing our song." Apollo got to his feet and held his hand out to her.

She didn't want to dance. She didn't feel like she belonged here in this scene right out of a fairy tale. Yet she couldn't turn Apollo down. He'd obviously worked so very hard on this evening. And he'd done an amazing job. He thought of everything, down to the finest detail.

And it would be so easy to be swept away into the romantic evening. But how could she do that when she knew how she'd gotten here? She was living her sister's life and being showered in baby smiles and giggles, when it was her sister who should be experiencing the joy of raising Seb.

The guilt weighed on her as she once again let Apollo guide her into his very strong, very capable arms. She lifted her gaze to thank him for such a wonderful evening, but when her gaze strayed across his mouth, she hesitated. Maybe it was the soft, lilting music in the background that had her thinking about lifting up on her tiptoes and pressing her lips to his. Or maybe it was the way his thumb stroked the small of her back.

As though he could read her thoughts, he lowered his head and caught her lips with his own. Her heart jumped to her throat. This is what she wanted—what she'd longed for all through dinner. She wanted to lean into him and let herself get swept away. His kiss was gentle and coaxing. And it'd be so easy to forget everything except the way it felt to be in his arms…but she couldn't.

It took all of her determination and a good amount of guilt to pull away from him. Though her heart and body yearned for the warmth of his touch and the heat of his kiss, she knew she couldn't do this. She didn't deserve this precious moment—a moment she'd gained at her sister's grave expense.

Apollo gazed at her with confusion reflected

in his eyes. "What's wrong? If I moved too fast... if I went too far—"

"No. It's not you. It's me." She realized the line was such a cliché, but that's because it was very accurate, especially in this instance. She lowered her gaze to the ground. "If only you knew what I've done."

Apollo stepped toward her and reached for her hand. "I can't imagine anything you've done that can be that bad."

"It's worse than bad." She pulled her hand away, refusing herself the comfort of his touch.

He cleared his throat. "Maybe you should tell me about it. Maybe we can figure out how to make it better."

She wished. Boy, did she wish. "It's not possible."

He led her over to a bench in the shadows and sat down. She didn't want to sit next to him because she knew if she did that the whole nightmare would come spilling out. But she'd had it bottled up for so long now. She should have told her mother, but what good would that have done? Her mother didn't deserve to be burdened with the truth—her truth. It wouldn't change anything. It wouldn't bring her sister back.

But Apollo was different. He was looking at her as though he wanted more from this relationship than a casual flirtation. And she wanted something more too—something like a real family, a family that her sister and brother-in-law should have had.

And she just couldn't let things go on like this.

"Talk to me, Popi." Apollo's voice was soft and comforting.

"You wouldn't be so nice to me if you knew the truth."

"Let me be the judge of that." When the staff approached to clear their dinner dishes, he sent them away. There was no one around now but him, her and the looming truth. His gaze searched hers. "I promise. Nothing you could say will be bad enough to put that look of worry on your face."

"You haven't heard my story yet."

"Then tell me."

She searched for what to say—how to begin. "I... I don't know how."

"Sure you do." He took her hand in his. His thumb lightly rubbed over her skin. "Start at the beginning."

Ever since the baby had been born, she'd been so busy, and at night so tired that she'd been able to push aside the haunting memories. But now that the baby was on a normal schedule and she was feeling better than ever, the guilt had been eating at her.

"It started at the beginning of spring." Her voice was unsteady as she attempted to keep her emotions in check. "My parents' fiftieth anniversary was approaching. You do know that my sister and I were adopted?" When he nodded, she continued. "My parents were childhood sweethearts and had married as soon as it was legal. But when they went to have kids, they found that they couldn't have them biologically. Which was lucky for my sister and me. But by the time my sister and I came along, our parents were older, not that it ever slowed them down."

Apollo remained silent, but she was certain that when he said start at the beginning, he hadn't meant to go this far back. But he'd realize shortly that it was all relevant. Or at least it had seemed so at the time.

"Anyway, with their golden anniversary quickly approaching, I wanted to do something super special for them—something they couldn't do for themselves."

"I'm sure anything you'd have done for them would have been appreciated."

"I know. But I wanted—no, I needed—this event to go above and beyond the norm. I wanted to show them just how much they meant to me and my sister. But Andrina was distracted with planning for the baby. I tried splitting up all of tasks that needed to be done for the party, but my sister kept forgetting to do this or that."

"Was this something unusual for her?"

Popi shrugged. "Not really. My sister wasn't much of a planner. She liked to do things spur of the moment. Day planners were foreign objects to her."

"And so she left all of the party preparations up to you?"

"Yes. But I was busy with the island weddings, plus I had morning sickness."

"You'd think your sister would be bending over backward to help you—what with you having her baby and all."

"She was in the beginning. I think as the thought of a baby became the reality of having a baby, she got jealous." Popi had never thought of it before, but looking back now as the pregnancy had progressed, Andrina had slipped into the shadows of her life. "It must have been so hard for her to face that I could have a baby when she couldn't."

"She's lucky to have a sister like you. Not everybody would step up and have a baby for their sibling. You are special."

Popi shook her head as though driving away his compliments. "Trust me. I'm not great."

"So, what happened? Did you two have a fight?"

"Yes. But it gets worse."

He tightened his hand around hers. "Go ahead. I promise nothing you say is going to drive me away."

"That's because you haven't heard it yet."

He placed a finger beneath her chin and lifted

her chin until their gazes me. "We'll work through this together. Just like on the island, we can do anything together."

She wanted to believe him. She truly did. But she knew this was going to be a game changer. And not in a good way, like the baby.

She drew in an unsteady breath as she turned her head to stare straight ahead into the black night. She just couldn't bear to witness the disappointment, the hurt and the anger that would surely cross his handsome face.

She drew in a calming breath. "I had a lot going on that day. I'd been dealing with a rather difficult client who had gone full-blown bridezilla on me. Not that there's any excuse for what I did." She sighed deeply in resignation that nothing would undo the past, no matter how much she wished that it were so. "And by the time I spoke with my sister that evening, I was exhausted and had little patience."

"I'm sure your sister understood. Everyone has had those days."

Popi shook her head. "Not like this. We were arguing over our parents' party—again. I felt like I was doing all the work. Calling the caterers. Setting up appointments with bands. Ordering invitations. You know. And my sister was just sitting back, letting me. She said that was because I was a party planner and I could do it better than her. When she said that, I lost it. I was tired of being taken for granted by her. Every time she needed something or when she didn't feel like doing something, she dumped it on her little sister. She'd been doing it all of our lives."

"I guess that's how Nile must have felt about me too. I was always ditching events to go off on a new adventure."

"But you had a legitimate excuse."

Apollo shrugged. "But was that reason enough to leave my brother to deal with everything from the family business to dealing with my very difficult father?"

"Your brother loved you."

"How do you know?"

"Because he never said a bad word about you and he wouldn't let anyone else speak ill of you."

Apollo's eyes widened. "Really?"

She nodded. "When he spoke of you, it was always positive."

"Even though I didn't deserve it." Apollo blinked away the moisture in his eyes. "Thanks for telling me. It means a lot."

"He'd tell you himself how much you meant to him…if he was still here. If that day had never happened."

"So, you and your sister were arguing. I still don't see how that has anything to do with the accident."

"Because I threatened my sister. I told her if she didn't go check out the private island for my parents to have their second honeymoon after the party that she would no longer be my sister. I had drawn a line in the sand—at the time, I was perfectly serious. And she knew it." Tears stung the back of Popi's eyes and she blinked repeatedly. "Why did I do it? Why did I have to give her that ultimatum?"

"Surely she knew you would forgive her. Is that what has you all upset? That you argued with her before she died?"

"No. It's that I forced her on the boat ride that killed her and your brother. Don't you see—if I hadn't made that threat, they wouldn't have been on that boat when it had a malfunction and blew up? It's all my fault."

Apollo got to his feet and knelt down in front of her. He reached up and swiped away a tear that streaked down her cheek. "It's no more your fault than it is mine."

She lifted her head. "How could it possibly be your fault? You weren't even here when it happened."

"Exactly. Maybe if I'd have been around, it would have changed the course of events. Maybe they wouldn't have been so distracted and would have researched the island sooner. Maybe your sister was so busy trying to keep up with my overworked brother and that was the reason she let so much work fall on your shoulders. Maybe in the end, the blame is mine."

"No. Don't say that. It isn't true. It's not your fault."

"Neither is it yours. I believe that when someone's time on earth is up, it doesn't matter where they are. It was the end of their time and there's nothing you or I could have done to change it. We both have to learn to accept it. The only thing we can do for them is to raise that little boy to the best of our ability and tell Seb about his biological parents. That's what they'd want us to do."

Popi blinked repeatedly. "Is that what you truly believe?"

"It is. And you deserve as much happiness as you can find in this world."

Without thinking, she asked, "With you?"

"I was hoping you'd want that." He reached up, his hand drawing her face to his. And then he kissed her. It was a kiss full of promise of all sorts of delights yet to come.

All too soon, he pulled back.

"Why did you stop?" she asked.

"I thought we'd have dessert up at the house."

"Dessert?"

A wicked smile lit up his face. "Dessert in bed. What do you think?"

"It doesn't get any better than that. Lead the way."

CHAPTER TWENTY

HE HADN'T SLEPT much the night before.

It was the best sleepless night of his life.

As the sun glowed brightly in the morning sky, Apollo was filled with energy and a sense of purpose. He'd slipped out of bed quietly to let Popi sleep. He'd fed Seb his breakfast, taken him for a stroll in the gardens and now Seb was back down for a midmorning nap.

Apollo sat down in the sunroom to drink some coffee and peruse the morning news. He'd been rolling around the idea of stepping up and running the family business for Seb. Now it was time to put his thoughts into action.

He had a degree in business that was about to get a workout as he eased back into the family business. He never thought he would be comfortable here at the estate, where he had so many bad memories, but Popi was helping him to make new memories—happy memories. And he never thought he'd be a businessman, but the thought of providing for his family appealed to him.

"What can I get you?" Anna, the housekeeper, asked.

He leaned back in his chair. "I'm thinking Popi should be up soon. How about lots of fresh fruit, eggs, pastries, the works."

Anna smiled brightly. "Am I to take it that she approved of your surprise?"

"Yes, she did." He'd always liked Anna. She'd always done her best by him. "Thanks for the suggestion."

"I'm just glad I could help. I'll go have the kitchen start your meal." She started to leave and then backed up. "Would you like me to wake Miss Popi?"

He continued to smile. "No need. I'll do it."

Just as Anna exited the room, his cell phone rang. He honestly wasn't in the mood for business today. Tomorrow was to be his first day in the office. But still, he checked the caller ID. When he found it was the number for a local merchant, he was about to send the call to his voice mail, but they didn't make a habit of calling him and curiosity got the better of him.

"Mr. Drakos, this is Manolas Decorating. Your nanny—or was it your decorator—was in here the other day, wanting to place a special order. We got the quote back from the manufacturer and it is quite costly. We wanted a verbal confirmation from you before we place the order."

"And this is for the nursery?"

"No, sir. I can't imagine that anyone would put this particular wallpaper in a child's room. Nor the flooring that was picked out. And there were some other items selected, as well."

"Just how much are we talking about?"

When the salesman spoke, Apollo sat straight up. That was more money than he'd allotted for the nursery. What was Popi thinking? And what was she planning to do with the supplies?

"No. Do not charge them to the account. There has been a mix-up." Apollo ended the call.

He sat there, staring blindly ahead. His friend's warning came back to him. Was it possible Popi was using him for the money? Would she use Seb to extort more money from the estate? Were these purchases just the beginning? Or was there truly some sort of misunderstanding?

"Sir, your mail." Anna placed a stack of envelopes on the table.

He didn't feel like sorting through it, but there was a large manila envelope that stuck out from all of the rest. In the corner was the address of an attorney located right here in Athens. A family law attorney. Popi's attorney.

He knew what was inside before he even opened the envelope. But like watching a horrible accident about to happen, he kept moving, letting the scene play out. Because he had to know the truth about Popi.

He removed the papers and scanned the top

sheet. It was the paperwork requesting Popi gain full and immediate custody of Seb. Apollo didn't have the stomach to read a list of reasons that he wasn't adequate to raise his nephew. He was about to toss aside the papers when he noticed at the bottom a request for support. This was something new. And the number was staggering.

The breath hitched in his throat. She wanted money.

He'd been so wrong about her.

And this time he wanted to be right—more than he'd ever wanted anything. He wanted Popi to be different than the other people that had let him down.

His hopes were dashed. He didn't know why he let people in, because in the end they hurt him every time. And he'd so wanted to believe in Popi—in what they'd shared. But now he was beginning to see what was important to her.

And it wasn't him.

Popi couldn't believe she'd slept so late.

But then again there hadn't been much sleeping going on during the night.

As soon as she entered the sunroom, she noticed that Apollo's mood had changed. The morning after was the awkward part. Maybe if she just acted like nothing had happened—like that was possible—things would eventually smooth out.

"Good morning." She flashed him a bright

smile, even though her insides shivered with nerves.

"Morning." His gaze didn't meet hers.

She took a seat next to him and poured herself a cup of coffee. Now that she was no longer pregnant and the baby wasn't breastfeeding, she was free to drink all the caffeine she desired—and this morning, she desired the entire pot. Every muscle in her body was sore, but in a good way—a very good way.

"You should have woken me to take care of Seb."

"No need."

She arched a brow. "You took care of him?"

A dark line formed across his brow. "Yes."

"Sorry. I just know how fussy he can get in the morning. And you've never handled him right when he wakes up. Did everything go okay?"

"Yes."

"That's good. I'll set my alarm for tomorrow." Her attempt at making conversation was failing miserably.

He turned his attention to his phone and appeared to be scrolling through emails. So much for pretending that last night didn't happen. She might as well face the big pink elephant in the middle of the room.

She took a sip of coffee before setting aside the cup. "About last night—"

"I don't want to talk about it."

When he looked at her, it was with skepticism and something else—was it anger? Or pain? But in a blink, his emotions were hidden behind a wall. She felt cutoff and adrift.

He regrets our night together.

When she'd confessed to her part in the death of her sister and his brother, Apollo had said all of the right things. In that moment, he'd convinced her that what had happened was fate. She should have known that once he thought over her confession about what had happened to his brother that he would blame her just like she blamed herself.

They'd let themselves get caught up in the moment—wanting to believe their attraction could overcome the obstacles. At least that's how it had been for her. Maybe for him it had been something much less—something more physical. Either way, it was over.

And there was the email that she'd received from Lea, confirming that the renovations to Infinity Island were almost complete. Popi's bungalow had been completed first and it was ready for her and Seb to return. She'd been planning to delay her return, just until she knew where things were going with Apollo. But now she knew and there was no reason to put off their departure. It was time to introduce Seb to his new home.

"I received an email this morning. The work on the island is wrapping up. It's time I leave."

Apollo's head lifted and his guarded gaze met hers. "It's probably for the best. Last night, it shouldn't have happened."

His words broke her heart. The breath stilled in her lungs as the pain of loss and rejection seeped into her bones. It was with effort that she sucked in some much-needed oxygen.

Just keep it together. Just a little longer.

"I... I slept too late to catch today's ferry. I still have all of my stuff to pack and the baby's—"

"He stays here." Apollo's blue eyes were ice-cold.

"I can't just leave him." Her voice wobbled.

This can't be happening. Everything is falling apart. All because I couldn't resist him last night.

Apollo placed both hands flat on the table and leaned toward her. "You're free to leave, but that little boy upstairs is my flesh and blood. Not yours. He stays."

His sharp words stabbed her heart. Was that what he'd boiled everything down to? Blood relations? Tears pricked the back of her eyes. She blinked. "But...he'll wonder what happened to me."

"I'm not heartless. I won't cut you completely out of his life." Apollo looked at her accusingly, like she'd do the same to him. "You can visit him here at the estate."

"And that's it?" She struggled to keep from shouting, but with every word her voice rose.

"I'm not the baby's biological aunt, so I'm not important—"

His gaze didn't meet hers. "I didn't say you weren't important."

"Just not as important as a Drakos." Anger, pain and resentment balled up within her. She felt like she was on the verge of losing absolutely everything that truly mattered to her. She couldn't just give up that precious baby boy. Not without a fight.

"What's wrong with being a Drakos?" Apollo's gaze lifted to meet hers. There was a challenge reflected in his icy-blue eyes. "My brother was a Drakos and he was a great man. The best man I've ever known."

Apollo was right on that point. Nile was a wonderful brother, from what she could tell, and an adoring husband. He would have made an amazing father if he'd had the chance. But there was something Apollo didn't seem to understand.

"It takes more than a name or blood ties to make a family." Her voice cracked with emotion. "It takes love—lots of it—and it takes time, one-on-one quality time. Without those you're nothing more than relatives—not a family."

Apollo stepped closer. His eyes flared with emotion. "I will always be that little boy's family. Don't you ever doubt it."

Popi had witnessed Apollo pull himself together over the past couple of months. She had

no doubt that if he put his mind to it, he would make a great father. With the passion he'd shown just now, she believed he would always be there for Seb. And no matter how upset Apollo was with her at the moment, he wouldn't keep her from having access to Seb.

In the end, she didn't want Seb constantly dragged back and forth between Infinity Island and the Drakos estate. Deep down she knew it was best for Seb to be settled in one place.

She attempted to tell Apollo that she would be back for regular visits with Seb, but when she opened her mouth, a lump of emotions blocked the words. Her heart was so full of love for her sister and for that little bundle upstairs that she'd been carrying around inside her for months. But she was also consumed with guilt for being the reason her sister and brother-in-law were on the boat. Maybe this was her penance.

Apollo got to his feet. "I'm needed at the office. I'll probably be in the city until late, so don't hold dinner for me. And my attorney will be in touch about visitation rights."

Without waiting for her to say a word and without a goodbye, he was gone. And Popi was left sitting alone, wondering what in the world had just happened in the last twenty-four hours. How could everything have gone from being so good—so happy—to this utterly desolate feeling?

CHAPTER TWENTY-ONE

SHOWERED AND DRESSED in a new suit, Apollo stepped in front of the floor-length mirror in his bedroom.

He didn't want to go to the office, especially a day early. But he couldn't just skulk around the house with Popi right here. He knew that sooner or later he would be drawn to her. He would want her to explain away the money and the custody papers. Like that could be done.

Why did he let himself think Popi was going to be different? Why did he think with her in his life that he could have a happy future? Happiness wasn't in the cards for him.

He moved to the table by the French doors, where fresh coffee had been left for him. He picked up the mug, knowing he would need some caffeine in order to get through the day. He took a drink, but it lacked its usual good taste.

The only thing he could do—his mission in life—was to look after his nephew. And he was going to throw all of his resources into blocking

Popi's attempt at gaining custody. Seb was a Drakos. He should grow up here in the family home.

And as upset as he was with Popi, he was mostly upset with himself. The thought of going after her—of ripping the baby out of her arms—sickened him. He set aside his coffee, no longer having the stomach for it.

Knock-knock.

"Come in."

Anna entered the bedroom, clucking her tongue and shaking her head just like she used to do when he would get in a row with Nile. He wanted to ignore her. He wanted to just sit here in his own puddle of self-pity. After all, he was the one who always came up with the short stick where relationships were concerned. Why didn't Anna sympathize with him instead of acting like he'd done something wrong?

"What is it?" His tone was short and curt.

She arched a brow at him and he suddenly regretted aiming his frustration at her. "I can't believe you are sending her away."

"I'm not sending anyone anywhere. Popi is leaving because she wants to. She can't get out the door fast enough."

"Uh-huh. You just keep telling yourself that."

Apollo got to his feet. "What is that supposed to mean?"

Anna crossed her arms as her determined gaze met his. "What else was she supposed to do with you being so closed off and short with her? This place was starting to feel like a home again. You were at last starting to be happy, just like I'd always wanted for you. What happened?"

Apollo turned away from Anna's probing eyes and moved to the window overlooking the garden—a garden he'd planted with Popi. "She wasn't the woman I thought she was."

"What sort of woman would that be?"

"One that cared." His voice was nothing more than a whisper.

"I think there's something you need to see."

"Not now. I just want to be left alone."

"It's important. Come with me and then if you want, I'll see that no one disturbs you the rest of the day."

He knew better than to argue with Anna. The woman was a force to be reckoned with, and it was easier and quicker to placate her than to argue the point.

He followed her to the other side of the house—the side that he made a point of avoiding. He didn't want to go there. He didn't know why Anna would take him here. She knew this part of the house had once been his father's sanctuary. For Apollo, it had been where he took his punishment for whatever his father felt like accusing him of that day.

He stopped. "Anna, I can't."

She turned to him. Determination gleamed in her eyes. "You must."

"Why? What's so important?"

"Something that just might change how you see the future." Without waiting for him to respond, she turned and kept walking.

Though every part of him wanted to turn and walk in the opposite direction, he found himself following Anna. What could possibly be so important?

As they walked, he noticed the hallway had been painted. Instead of that dingy dark gray color that had adorned these halls all his childhood, they were now a much cheerier off-white. And the portrait of ancient wars was replaced with portraits of landscape scenes. Where had they come from? Was this something that Popi had splurged on?

They turned a corner and stopped in front of a set of double doors. Anna turned to him. "I wasn't supposed to show you this. It was meant to be a surprise but under the circumstances, I thought you should see what Popi has been up to while the baby naps."

Anna pushed open the doors and then stepped aside. Why would Anna let Popi mess around in this room? Anna knew the bad memories he had in here. But when he stepped inside the room, the big oak desk where his father would sit and drink his bourbon was gone. In its place was a modern glass desk. Everything in the room was light and bright—something his father would have hated. And greenery was everywhere. The bookcases that had lined the wall behind his father's desk were gone. The wall was blank as though it wasn't finished.

Knock-knock.

He turned to find two delivery men with a big roll in their arms, plus some other supplies.

The men paused at the doorway. "We're from Manolas Decorating with a delivery."

Apollo was confused. "But I refused payment."

The man looked at the paper in his hand. "It says that it was paid in full. A Miss Costas paid."

And it had to be with her own funds.

While the man placed the supplies off to the side of the room, Apollo tried to make sense of everything. The money Popi had spent had been for him. She was trying to wipe away the sadness of the past and paint him a new future full of light and hope.

If he was wrong about her and the money, what else had he been wrong about?

The memory of the custody papers sitting on the table haunted him. How could that be a misunderstanding? Popi had to know what she was doing.

But another part of him wanted to believe there was an explanation he hadn't thought of.

He couldn't leave things like this. He needed answers before it was too late.

He retrieved the custody papers and headed for Popi's room. He rapped his fingers on the door, hoping she was there. Surely she wouldn't have slipped away to a hotel or anything. To his relief, the door opened.

Popi's normally bright and sparkly eyes were dulled and red. Had she been crying? Because her plans were about to go awry? Or was it something more?

He held up the papers. "Was this your idea?"

"Was what my idea?" Confusion reflected in her eyes.

"To sue me for custody of Seb and to ask for large support payments?"

"What?" She paused as though making sense of what he was saying. "Can I see those?"

"You don't know what they say?"

She frowned at him. "Obviously I don't or I wouldn't ask to see them."

Hope started to swell in his chest, but he tamped it down. It was too soon and he still had questions. "Then why else would your attorney send me these papers?"

Popi sighed and turned to walk farther into her room. "Because I accidentally overheard you on the phone. You were making plans to leave on a safari—another one of your dangerous adventures. And…and I wanted to make sure the baby is with me when you're out of town."

"I'm not going anywhere. I'm not sure what you heard, but my life is here with Seb." He stopped himself from saying that his life was with her too, because he still had unanswered questions. "I have no intention of leaving Seb. And I told my friend exactly that."

"Oh, I didn't know."

He had one more important question. "And the really large support payments?"

"I don't know anything about those. I called my attorney and I was a bit worked up at the time. I told her to do what was best. I thought she would send the papers to me first—not you."

His gaze searched her eyes, finding nothing but honesty reflected in them. He knew that his next move would determine the ultimate fate of their relationship.

"I have to go."

He turned and exited the room. His mind was already churning through this new information and what it meant.

He didn't have time to bask in the hope that filled him. Instead he needed to act. His questions had been satisfactorily answered, but he couldn't just apologize and expect Popi to give up her life on Infinity Island. He had to give her a reason to stay here—with him.

* * *

Goodbyes were so hard.

Popi's dream of raising Seb alongside Apollo had been dashed. That acknowledgment slashed through her heart. How had she read everything with Apollo so wrong?

As she stood in the dimly lit nursery, Popi blinked repeatedly, stemming the river of tears threatening to spill onto her cheeks. If she gave into her emotions now, she didn't think she'd be able to stop crying.

It was time for her to head back to the island… back to her job…back to the welcoming embrace of the island's close-knit community. Seb would be loved and cared for here. Apollo would see that this precious baby had a hands-on, adoring father. Of that she had absolutely no doubts.

Raised as a Drakos, Seb would have every opportunity to live a fantastic life. And once a formal visitation agreement was drawn up, she'd see Seb every single chance she was allowed. She'd be around so much that he'd get tired of seeing her, but she would never get enough of Seb's smiles and laughter.

She held Seb in her arms until he fell asleep. Tears clouded her vision. She whispered, "You will be safe here. Your uncle will see to it. You will be loved by Apollo and Anna and the rest of the staff that think you hung the stars." When

Shadow meowed from his spot atop the chest of drawers, Popi smiled through her tears. "And Shadow will love…" Her voice cracked. "He'll love you too."

She blinked repeatedly as unshed tears clouded her vision. If she didn't leave now, she was afraid that she wouldn't have the strength to do the right thing—leave Seb here. This was his home—his destiny. She'd watched Apollo over the past weeks and he was up to being a good father.

"I love you, little guy." She placed the sleeping baby in the crib. "Your mum and dad are watching over you. Always. And I'll be back just as soon as I can." She swiped the tears from her cheeks.

And then she slipped an envelope from her purse and placed it against the lamp on the chest of drawers. With all her things packed and the baby down for the night, there was nothing left to do but leave.

With every step she took toward the door, it felt like her heart was being ripped from her chest. Without allowing herself to glance back, she exited the mansion and walked down the long driveway, to where a taxi was waiting to take her to a hotel for the night. Tomorrow she would catch the ferry back to Infinity Island—where she belonged.

CHAPTER TWENTY-TWO

WOULD THIS WORK?

The next morning, after a few hours of restless sleep, Apollo had his plan in motion. It was the only thing he could think of to change Popi's mind about leaving—about leaving him for being such a jerk.

Apollo had to admit, for a man used to making decisive decisions in the spur of the moment with potentially deadly consequences, he was totally unsure about this one. Would it be enough to convince her to stay?

The one thing he did know was that she had changed things for him. Little things and big things. And if he didn't do everything he could to keep her from walking out that door for good, he would lose his chance at happiness. He was certain of that.

He'd heard it said by the elders that there was one true love in the world for each person. Popi was that person for him. And he had to show her that a future with him was worth pursuing. But would she believe him?

It was time to find out. He went to her room and knocked on the door. There was no answer. After he knocked again and called out her name, he opened the door. Her bed was made up as though it hadn't been slept in. He checked the bathroom, finding no sign of her things. The closet was empty. The dresser was empty.

She was gone.

But why? It was way too early to catch the ferry.

And then his thoughts turned to Seb. Had they both slipped away without even so much as a goodbye? His chest tightened. That couldn't be. Popi wouldn't do that, would she?

Apollo rushed down the hallway to the nursery. He barreled through the doorway and came to a halt when he saw Seb in the crib, kicking his feet and smiling up at his mobile.

Apollo rushed over and picked up the baby. "Thank goodness you're still here. That means Popi must still be here. I have to find her."

It was then that his gaze strayed across the white envelope on the dresser with his name on it. He knew that writing. It was Popi's. His heart sunk down to his loafers.

He called for the nanny. Once the baby was tended to, he took the envelope and walked back

to his room. He didn't want to be disturbed when
he read what Popi had to say to him.

Apollo,
I'm sorry for disrupting your life in so many
ways. I'm sorry for so many things these
days. The one thing I'm not sorry for is having Seb and getting a chance to see you with
him. You are going to be such a great father.
Seb will thrive under your care.
   I'm going back to where I belong—back
to Infinity Island. In the morning, I will contact my attorney and have the custody case
withdrawn. Seb belongs with you.
Take care of yourself,
Popi

Things couldn't end this way. He had to find
her. He had to prove to her that they were better
together than apart.

Life would be better once she returned to Infinity Island.

That's what Popi had told herself all night—a
very long night. Memories of Apollo kept coming one after the other. She missed the sound of
his voice, the twinkle in his eyes when he smiled
at her and most of all she missed the utter bliss of
feeling his arms around her.

But once she made it back to the island, she

would be busy. There would be so much to do to get the wedding business back up and operating. There would be receptions to plan. People to talk to. And lots to keep her mind from straying to the two men who meant the world to her.

Leaving was for the best. And she couldn't take a baby away from his doting uncle and the home that belonged to him. They would get along fine without her—she couldn't bear to think it would be otherwise.

And maybe someday soon, Apollo would find love—

She halted her thoughts there. The thought of him with someone else was just too painful to contemplate. The best she could do at the moment was to hope he found happiness.

The long, low blow of the ferry whistle let her know it was time to move to the dock. And yet she didn't move. She didn't want to move.

The truth was she'd been happy in Athens with Apollo and Seb. Happier than she'd ever been in her life. Her mind began to replay snippets of memories, from their walks in the garden to their shared meals to their candlelit dinner, where they danced beneath the stars. That had been such a perfect night. Too perfect.

The truth was she had no right to be so happy. How was she supposed to have the perfect family and the perfect life when her sister had been robbed of her happiness? Life was not fair. Not at all.

Popi didn't know how long that she'd sat there when someone bumped her suitcase and jarred her back to reality. She needed to get on that ferry before it pulled out without her. And then she'd have to spend another night alone in a hotel room, with nothing but her memories and regrets to keep her company.

She got up from the bench and lifted the handle on her suitcase. She started to roll it toward the busy dock when she thought she heard her name being called out. She glanced around but didn't see anyone she recognized. It was probably her imagination, combined with her abysmal night's sleep.

"Popi! Wait!"

That time she was certain of what she'd heard. It was Apollo's voice. She stopped and turned, but there were so many people behind her. And they were none too happy that she had stopped and held them up.

She should keep going. There was nothing left for them to say to each other. But then she thought of Seb. Maybe there was something wrong. She worried her bottom lip for a moment and then got out of line.

Apollo approached her. "We need to talk."

"Is it Seb?"

"Don't worry. He's fine."

"Then I have to go." She couldn't bear to drag this out any further. The pain of loss was still so deeply etched in her heart. "Please leave me alone."

"Not until we talk." His tone brooked no compromise.

She turned to him, pleading with her eyes. "You don't know how hard leaving was for me. I just can't drag this out."

"Not even for Seb's sake?"

Worry for herself ceased. "Is Seb all right?"

"Yes. I didn't mean to imply otherwise. But he misses you. He wants you to come back. Let's talk."

She gave a determined shake of her head. "There's nothing left to say. It's time I go home." She turned to walk to the end of the long line of people heading for the dock. Some people were day laborers. Others were heading out on boats bound for various destinations. And some were like her and going home—at last.

"Popi," he reached for her arm. "Please don't walk away. Not until you've heard what I have to say."

She didn't know what he could say that would make a difference. Surely he'd read her note that she wasn't going to fight him for custody of Seb. Even if she wanted to, she didn't have the resources to challenge his deep pockets. But she still planned to have regular access to her nephew.

She hadn't written that in the note. She'd been too worked up at the time to think to include it. Maybe now was the time to make it clear that she wasn't totally backing out of Seb's life. She wanted a binding agreement written by their attorneys.

She turned back to him. "I'm listening."

"Not here." He glanced around at the crowd of people. "How about over there?" He pointed to a vacant bench off to the side of the marina.

She followed him to the bench and sat down. She turned to him, knowing she had to say this quickly before she lost her nerve. "Before you say anything, I want you to know that I'm not abandoning Seb. I still plan to be a part of his life and visit him as much as possible. I think that's what my sister would have wanted under the circumstances. I can tell him about his mother. Things that no one else would know."

Apollo stared into her eyes. "I would never keep you from Seb."

"Thank you." Her heart was breaking as they were talking. All she wanted was for this conversation to be over. It was too painful to be this close and yet this far away from him. "I should go."

"Not yet."

The truth was she didn't understand why he was here. She'd given him everything he'd wanted—a life with Seb. There was nothing left for her to give.

A couple blasts of the ferry whistle let her know the boat was about to pull out. But not without her. She had to get back to Infinity Island.

She jumped to her feet. "I've got to go."

She rushed toward the dock. She sensed Apollo behind her. Why was he being so insistent? Was he afraid he couldn't handle the baby on his own? That was just nerves. Seb loved him. And so did she…

The thought sent a wave of fresh pain coursing through her body. Her feet moved faster. Apollo was right behind her. How was she supposed to get over him when he wouldn't go away?

Apollo was speaking but with the crush of people and the sounds of the dock, she couldn't make out his words—she didn't want to make them out. She wanted to forget that she ever knew him—though she knew that would be utterly impossible.

When she finally made it through the congestion and reached the end of the dock, the walkway had been drawn up. The ferry was just beginning to pull out.

"Wait!" This couldn't be happening. "Please. I need on the boat."

"Sorry," yelled a young sailor. "You'll have to catch the ferry tomorrow."

"But please. It's important."

"Can't stop the ferry now."

Popi was so anxious to get away from Apollo that, for a moment, she considered swimming for the boat. But she knew that would cause pandemonium, and the water wasn't exactly inviting right next to the dock. It was murky, unlike the clear blue water on the island.

With a resigned sigh, she leveled her shoulders and turned. She knew Apollo would be standing there. What was it going to take to make him go away?

Her gaze met his and her heart thump-thumped like it did every time he stared deep into her eyes. "Say whatever it is you have to say and then be on your way."

"I'd rather show you."

"Show me what?"

"Come with me."

She hesitated. "I… I don't think that's a good idea."

"How about we make a deal?"

"What sort of deal?"

"You come with me and if you don't like what I have to show you, I will chopper you out to the island today. You won't have to spend another night on the mainland."

That deal was too good to pass up. But what did he have to show her that was so important?

CHAPTER TWENTY-THREE

THIS HAS TO WORK.

Apollo wanted this more than he'd wanted anything in his life.

And he was more nervous than he had been while crossing the Amazon with its many dangers.

"What are we doing back here?" Popi asked.

"You'll see." He drove past the front of the house, toward the back.

"Apollo, what's going on?" Popi stared out the window at the big white tent he'd erected the night before. "If this is some sort of party—"

"It's not. I promise."

He got out of the car and came to her side. He opened the door and offered her a hand out but she didn't accept it. She got out on her own.

"But I don't understand." She walked to the edge of the drive. "The gardens look like they are set up for a wedding." She turned to him. The color faded from her face. "Are you trying to tell me you're getting married?"

"I'm not. At least not right now. I put this together for you."

She pressed a hand to her chest. "For me? But I'm not getting married."

"Come see. And then I'll explain."

He held out his arm to her. She hesitated at first, but then slipped her hand into the crook of his arm. He led her down the aisle. And in that moment, he knew without any shadow of a doubt that he was doing the right thing. They belonged together. But how did he convince Popi of that?

At the end of the aisle, he turned to her. "I did this for you. I wanted to show you that Infinity Island isn't the only place for beautiful weddings."

Confusion reflected in her eyes.

He cleared his throat. "I'm not saying this very well. What I mean is that you could—if you wanted, that is—run a wedding business right here at the estate."

"But why?"

He gazed deep into her beautiful brown eyes, willing her to truly hear what he was saying. "Because I want you to stay. I've made such a mess of things. I wasn't expecting to fall in love with you—"

"You love me?"

He smiled and nodded. "I think I have since we danced at your friend's wedding. But I didn't know it at the time. And then after we made love,

I panicked and I let my doubts and insecurities overrule what I knew about you."

"Which is?"

"That you are beautiful both inside and out. That you would do anything for the people you love—even sacrificing your happiness."

"I can't believe you're saying all of this…even after the part I played in the deaths of our siblings."

He stepped closer to her and brushed the back of his fingers gently down over her cheek. She couldn't resist leaning into him and drawing on his strength.

His gaze met hers. "You have to stop blaming yourself. You didn't do anything wrong. Sometimes bad things happen and there's no one to blame."

"Really?" Hope gleamed in her eyes.

"Really. Quit being so hard on yourself. It isn't what your sister would want."

Popi paused as though considering his words. He was right. This not what Andrina would want. "My sister could procrastinate with the best of them, but she was never vindictive."

"See. The only one who has to forgive you… is you."

Popi nodded in understanding. "I'll work on it."

He was winning her over—he was certain of it. "So, what do you say? Would you like to stay here with me—with Seb? And start your own wedding business?" And then he realized he'd forgotten something. "And that tent off to the side, it's going to become a conservatory with glass walls and ceiling so you can dance beneath the stars. And you may use it for your weddings. Use whatever you desire."

"You'd do all of that?"

He nodded. "And more, if you'll say yes. I've traveled the world searching for something— something I never found. Until now. I've found my home right here with you and Seb." He pulled a ring from his pocket and dropped down on one knee. "I love you, Popi, with all of my heart. Will you be my partner on the biggest and grandest adventure of my life?"

Tears splashed onto her cheeks. "I will. I love you."

EPILOGUE

Five months later...
The Drakos Estate, Athens, Greece

THIS WAS GOING to be the wedding of the season.

Every newspaper, television network and paparazzo was in attendance.

But the guest list was quite selective—only family and friends.

And so the media was left outside the gates. But that didn't stop them from hiring helicopters to whirl above the big white tent in the lawn of the Drakos estate. But with a few well-placed calls, Apollo was able to get the helicopters removed, letting the peaceful chirp of the birds and the rustle of the wind be the only backdrop to this occasion.

In just a few hours, Popi was going to become Mrs. Apollo Drakos. And then the adoption of Seb would become official. Popi moved to the crib and lifted her future son into her arms.

Popi held Seb so that she could look him in his

eyes. "Very soon Apollo and I will be your legal parents. But don't worry, we'll make sure you know all about your very special birth parents. They loved you so much. We all do."

"What's going on in here?" Apollo's voice came from the doorway.

Popi turned to him. "You aren't supposed to see the bride before the wedding. It's bad luck."

He stepped farther into the room and didn't stop until he was next to her. He planted a quick kiss on her lips and then one on the baby's forehead. "We don't need luck. We have love on our side."

Aww... This was one of the reasons that she'd fallen in love with him. Once he'd trusted her enough to let down his guard, she'd found an optimistic side to him. And Apollo truly believed what he said. And she believed in him. They didn't need luck, because their love was strong enough to see them through anything.

The smile slipped from his face. "I just have one question for you."

"What's that?"

"Are you sure about starting your own wedding business here? I will understand if you want to return to Infinity Island." He gazed deeply into his eyes. "My home is wherever you are." At that point, the baby let out a cooing sound. Their gazes moved to Seb. "And you too, little guy."

"And my home is here." With her free hand,

Popi reached out to Apollo. Her fingers traced down over the stubble trailing down his jaw. "My heart belongs to you. And I can't wait to start my own business. I've already been working on a new website and deciding what colors I'll use for my brand."

"You have?" When she nodded, he said, "I can't believe you've had time with all our wedding plans, the baby and finishing the remodel. I'm so proud of all you accomplished in such a short amount of time. You are amazing."

She smiled. When he talked to her that way, she felt as though she could accomplish anything. It meant so much that he believed in her.

Before she could put her thoughts into words, there was a knock at the door. Lea stepped into the room with the newest addition to their group. Baby Lily was in her arms, sound asleep.

Lea smiled. "Hey, you two aren't supposed to be together before the wedding."

Popi nodded toward her soon-to-be-husband. "Someone says that we don't have to worry about luck."

"Really?" There was disbelief in her voice. "I wouldn't want to tempt fate." She narrowed her gaze on Apollo. "That means you need to go." When he didn't make any move to go, she added, "Now."

Popi turned to Apollo. "I think she's serious. You better go."

He sighed. "But the wedding isn't for hours."

"You'll be fine." Lea smiled once more. "I've never seen a more perfect couple."

"She's right," Popi said. "It's only three more hours—"

"And three minutes," Apollo added.

"In three hours...and three minutes, I'll be all yours. And you can have me all evening."

"Mmm... I like the sound of that." He leaned in close and pressed his lips to hers.

"Hey! Hey! Hey!" Lea said. "You have to wait for that until after the vows."

Apollo groaned as he pulled away. "It won't come soon enough." And then he looked at Seb. "I will see you soon, little guy. Hopefully you haven't outgrown your tux."

"We just got the outfit for him last week," Popi said.

"He's a Drakos. He's growing quickly."

"Don't rush him. I'm enjoying having a baby."

"Me too." His gaze sought hers out. "Maybe we should discuss having another one."

"Really?"

"Mmm-hmm." His gaze reflected his sincerity.

Lea moved between them and, with her free arm, gave Apollo a shove toward the door. "It's definitely time you go. Out. Out."

When Apollo closed the door behind him, Lea turned to her. "Wow. That guy is really crazy about you."

"It goes both ways."

"I'm really going to miss you on the island. But I totally understand why you want to stay here. You have a devoted guy. And this mansion and the grounds are amazing."

"Apollo created the garden where we're getting married. Together, we're turning this into our home with our memories."

"Then we better start getting you ready. We have a blissful memory to make."

"Yes, we do."

This was just the beginning of the greatest love story. Popi smiled. She never knew life could be this good. And it was all due to Apollo. She loved him with all her heart.

"Popi, come on." Lea placed Lily in the crib. "You have to put down Seb. We have to get you ready for your groom. It's almost time for you to say 'I do.'"

Popi's feet barely touched the ground.

There really were happily-ever-afters…

* * * * *